Moony's
Road to Hell

Moony's Road to Hell

Manuel Ramos

University of New Mexico Press

Albuquerque

F

Library of Congress Cataloging-in-Publication Data

Ramos, Manuel.

Moony's road to hell / by Manuel Ramos.

p. cm.

ISBN 0-8263-2949-7 (cloth : alk. paper)

1. Private investigators—Colorado—Denver—Fiction.

2. Mexican Americans—Fiction.   3. Denver (Colo.)—Fiction.

4. Drug traffic—Fiction.   I. Title.

PS3568.A4468 M66 2002

813'.54—dc21

2002002836

Justice is turned back,

And righteousness stands afar off;

For truth is fallen in the street,

And equity cannot enter.

So truth fails,

And he who departs from evil makes himself a prey.

Isaiah 59:14–15

Kiko Vigil nursed a warm beer in the semidarkness of La Tortuga. Tonight he kept his promise, even if it was only to himself. He had to level with Lorraine. He had screwed up. He could never arrest her. He might scare her away, hope that she would leave and never return to Denver. He would not be the man who finally finished Elías Garza.

The noise never stopped in La Tortuga. *Banda* music from a jukebox bounced off the walls and roared back at Kiko. Customers were forced to yell and gesture to communicate the most basic messages. *"¿Quieres otra?"* "Wanna dance, baby?" The shouting mixed in with sounds of breaking glass, doors slammed shut, the thud of bodies tossed against a wall. Smoke hung in heavy clouds at eye level, and in the background a light swinging over a pool table was interrupted by the shadows of men who played eight ball.

Tubas, trumpets, guitars, and accordions congealed into a beat that on another night would have had the burly, handsome man kicking up his boots and hollering his fool ass off just like any drunk *mexicano* in the joint. Couples were doing exactly that all around him. He fidgeted in a booth at the back of the room where he waited for Lorraine.

Vigil blamed his headache on the smoke and noise, but he knew it was more than that. An undercover agent for the Immigration and Naturalization Service was sworn to prevent violations of the U.S. immigration laws and to apprehend those who flouted those laws, whether they were pathetic illegals who crossed over dreaming about a new pickup truck that would surely be theirs after a week or so of work or the organized gangsters who made millions of dollars from the flow of undocumented aliens and illegal drugs. He had violated his own code, for Lorraine. And she wasn't a pathetic illegal.

Kiko knew Lorraine had walked in the bar before he saw her. Every man in the place turned and watched her long strides cross the grimy floor to the booth. Some stared openmouthed and made the vulgar remarks that certain Mexican men will make whenever they are in the presence of any woman other than their mother. Others averted their eyes as soon as they had focused on the face, either because they were embarrassed by the thoughts that such a face generated or they knew the face, recognized it as the property of Elías Garza. Mrs. Garza was strictly off-limits, and only the dumbest *baboso* would try to hit on her.

She slid in the booth across from Vigil and placed her well-manicured fingers over his hands, clasped together as though he were praying. Her smile broke through the smoke and dimness, and Kiko expelled a rush of air from his tight lungs. Even then, even when he stared at the disaster of his life, she excited him, brought out his desire and heat.

She spoke to him in excited Spanish. "Kiko, baby. I thought you wouldn't be here. You've been acting so strange lately. What is it? What's wrong? Why didn't you come to my house? This bar—I hate this place. You know that. These men here, they act like animals. Even Elías doesn't come here. He can't stand these people."

He flinched. She said her husband's name to her lover without hesitation, brought him up in the conversation as though he were just another acquaintance, a person they both knew and so they both could talk about him.

Kiko Vigil clutched her fingers like a falling man grasping at lifelines. Lorraine's husband was the number-two man, answerable only to Placido Cardoza, the real boss back home in Guadalajara. In the United States, Garza held all the cards and pulled all the strings. Lorraine Garza was as involved as her husband.

Her life would be worthless, but her death would be lucrative for the killer who accepted Garza's inevitable offer to pay for vengeance. Her affair with Kiko would be revealed in the courtroom. If she escaped, the missing Lorraine Garza would bring questions from Vigil's superiors, and those questions would lead to this night when he warned her, when he blew his cover and jeopardized months of work that had already cost the lives of one agent and at least three smugglers—coyotes—who had raised the suspicions of Elías Garza.

"Lorraine, listen. This is very important. I have to tell you something, and you have to understand. This is the last time for us, for us together. It has to be."

She didn't let him go on. She said, "I won't hear this. You know how I feel about you, and you feel the same about me. I know it. I don't care about Elías like that any-more. We have to be together—there's no other way. And now that Elías wants to give you more responsibility for some of the fieldwork, that means we can be together most of the time. Elías doesn't want to do the work—he's been looking for someone to turn it over to. He knows I can do it, but they won't let a woman run things. You and I can do it together. He will go back to Guadalajara and join Cardoza. He won't even miss me—you must believe me."

The words rushed out. He tried to stop her, to tell her that she had it all wrong, but she wouldn't listen. Maybe she knew what he was about to reveal and was trying to prevent it, all the while recognizing the futility of her efforts.

A ripple of movement caught the corner of his left eye. A man dressed in a dark suit and black shirt emerged from the smoke and noise and quickly made his way to the back of the bar. Vigil had made a turn to get the man in full view when the first shot tore open his chest and exploded his aorta. He slammed against the booth and twitched in agony as blood flooded his lungs. The next bullets were irrelevant to their purpose. Kiko Vigil was dead before the man slit Kiko's throat and left the knife embedded in Kiko's shat-tered chest. He was dead before the man grabbed the screaming, hysterical Lorraine and hauled her away with Kiko's blood dripping from her long hair. And Francisco Kiko Vigil died long before the police rushed into the deserted bar and found him sprawled on the floor with a piece of paper stuck to the knife blade. On the paper were the neatly printed words:

Quien todo lo quiere todo lo pierde.

2

"**Y**ou got the look, the talk, and the attitude of a cop—a government agent. You even got the smell of a cop."

Robert Spann nodded. Almost three decades of habit and routine had engraved upon his soul and body the trappings of federal law enforcement, from mirror shiny black shoes, to boring gray suits, to gray crew cut. The image had taken time to fully emerge, but the frame for the eventual picture had been there all along.

"Nothing I can do about it. Even the brass asses decided years ago I could never work undercover."

Danny Mora, the private investigator, knew all about Robert Spann. Only on rare occasions had any type of cop asked for Mora's help, so when one of the veterans of the INS called for an appointment, Mora learned all he could about his visitor.

In the 1960s, Spann had been a youthful spit-and-polish U.S. Marshal with more patriotism than brains. From security duty at federal courthouses to escorting mob snitches to their witness protection hideouts, Spann had enjoyed an interesting two decades behind the marshal's badge. But when his seniority and the rigid bureaucracy of the marshal's office had threatened Spann with a desk job, he began a feverish scramble for something else in the field, out where there was still enough action to keep a man young, as he liked to repeat to his cronies who had opted for the calm lassitude of windowless offices. Eventually he finagled an interagency transfer to the INS, *la migra.*

As far as Mora had learned, Spann had no special antipathy for the illegals. He wasn't heartless, not a law-and-order robot.

His years as a bodyguard for federal judges who demanded all the trappings that befitted their regal posts or on patrol in the Arizona desert searching for clumps of skittish humanity had taught him how to sense when a man was lying to him, or not telling the whole truth, or when a set of circumstances didn't quite come off right.

And now, because of his ability to read the weaknesses of his fellow human beings, Robert Spann found himself sitting on a hard-backed wooden chair in the office of a man for whom he had no fondness and quite a bit of apprehension—the only man who could help Robert Spann at this particular point in his life.

Mora said, "Don't take that the wrong way. It's been a long time, Bob. What, maybe five, six years?"

Mora's large face stared directly at Spann. The clear dark

eyes refused to blink, and Spann looked away to the wooden and ceramic masks hanging on the wall behind Mora.

From somewhere in central and southern Mexico, Mora had salvaged ritual objects from rural villages. More than a dozen of the masks watched Spann. A bat's head with long, curved ears and the carved impression of a human face behind the bat laughed alongside something that could have been a dragon, but Spann wasn't sure. What else could have a mouth from which protruded two frogs, ears that transformed into serpents, an oversized, bulbous notched nose, and eyes that sparkled with the fire of a devil's joke?

A woman's red face smiled at Spann. The blemishes on her immodest crimson cheeks made him cringe when he realized that they were small lizards desperately clinging to her skin. Mora had created a montage of protruding tongues, grotesque half-human, half-animal beings, and tiny menacing creatures.

A bookcase under the masks had four well-stocked shelves, without any apparent cohesiveness to the layout of the books—paperbacks and hardbacks—except that they all appeared to be well read. Used and reused. Spann didn't recognize the titles. *The Silver Cloud Café. The Drunken Boat. . . . y no se lo tragó la tierra. The Poet in New York. White Leg.*

Spann's nose wrinkled at a hint of smoke. He worried for an instant until he convinced himself that the musky smell must be an artificial scent that Mora had for his office.

The last time the two men had spoken to each other, Robert Spann had refused to answer any of Mora's questions. Mora had been a fresh face, an inexperienced private investigator who could be bluffed by the hard tone and gruff manner of a federal lawman. Both men had changed since then.

Robert Spann rubbed the palm of his left hand across the short nub of hair at the base of his neck. He was due for a haircut, he thought.

He said, "Yeah, it's been a few years. Funny, we never ran up against each other again. But I've heard about some of your cases. That's why I want to hire you. Only thing is, I've got to know ahead of time that whatever you find out, whatever happens, that's between you and me only, right? Unless I say otherwise."

The detective said, "I'm not much of a fan of the INS. And if you think you can't trust me, you're probably right. I doubt we can work with each other."

Spann pursed his lips and stretched his pale, scrawny neck. He needed Mora.

"Look, I didn't mean it the way it sounded. I'm sure you respect your clients' confidences. This thing is hard for me. I can't seem to get a handle on what the hell I really want. So, it's not you I'm worried about. I guess it's me. If you find out something that rocks everything I think I know and understand, then, then I, uh, I'm not sure how I'll handle it. That's what I mean. It's not you."

Mora loosened the tie he had worn for the testimony he had provided earlier in the day. Spann eventually had to spit out whatever it was that had brought him to the office of a private investigator. Sometimes clients couldn't wait to spill every small detail of the very personal crisis that had forced them to bring in a stranger to probe those sensitive details. Others wanted Mora to guess at why they were sitting in his clean and neat office. They would talk about almost anything except their business, admire the fact that there wasn't a file out of place, not a stray pencil on any surface, not even a wad of paper in the trash can. He would finally ask what they wanted, prod them to get it out, and then they would break down, sometimes with shame and regret and sometimes with gleeful rancor now that they knew they were on the road to getting even, as long as Mora did his job.

Mora was sticky and tired. A fan blew warm air across the back of his stale shirt, but it didn't help his funk.

Through his office window he watched a thunderstorm move over the city. Thunderheads rolled above the down-town buildings, and lightning cracked open the sky. The heat wave had been broken, temporarily, now that the city was baked and dried out.

He listened, and Spann's words immediately triggered in him the old response that he loved, the reason that he kept an office where he had to worry about rent, parking for clients, and screening his own calls when he could have found nice, steady employment in any one of the national agencies that had set up regional offices in Denver or with a corporation where the pay and expense account would really mean something. But the jobs in those places wouldn't give him that feeling, that urge that made him want to go out and start talking to people, to visit and loiter at the crime scene, to work over a plan of surveillance and determine who else was needed for the job. Mora liked the stories that walked into his downtown office. The kind of story and people and events that Robert Spann described in a quiet voice, a pro-fessional voice muted with years of experience, but a voice that broke occasionally because Robert Spann wasn't heartless, he wasn't a robot, and he was a man who understood completely what it meant to call another man friend.

"My best friend, Kiko Vigil, was the agent killed six months ago. The agency laid his killing on his own head—said that he got involved with a woman, got careless, and died because he couldn't keep his pants on. I think there's more to it than that. I want the whole story out. There might even have been a cover-up. Kiko Vigil was a good man, the best agent I ever knew. He saved my life. He died an ugly death. I owe it to him to get the story straight. I want you to find the truth for me."

The afternoon shower had dampened the earth until it glistened with promise and potency. Moisture hung in the air, stirring a breeze that caressed and soothed. The night was perfect for a loud, music-rich party under backyard lights where people talked in animated groups, laughing couples twirled in melodramatic dances, and the food and liquor flowed as freely as the camaraderie.

Tomás Chávez had come alone to the party. Lydia rarely accompanied him to these kinds of events. He realized they seldom did anything together anymore. Whatever it meant to be a couple didn't apply to his wife and him. They had ceased being a couple so long ago that he had convinced himself that he was more comfortable when he was alone, without her.

The hostess, Silvia, had danced almost every dance since

the serious music had started. The Mexican *rancheras* of tried-and-true legends, rhythm and blues for the younger generation from a hot New Orleans group, and fifties rock and roll compelled her to approach almost every man present and insist that he dance with her. Her husband, Charles, laughed and slapped the men on their backs as they were led to the concrete dance floor by his beautiful wife, and he would shout, "Dance, hombre, dance! This is your chance. It's her party and she loves to dance."

No one thought anything about the haphazard exchange of partners except, perhaps, that Silvia was a dancing fool, a woman who knew how to enjoy the celebration of one more year of togetherness. Silvia and Charles were a fun pair; all their friends said that. But Charles was concerned that his guests have enough food and drink, that they were laughing or talking seriously about the matters that were important for this group of people, and that they would remember this anniversary party as one of the best. Those concerns kept Charles busy for many of the tunes that begged for dancers, forcing Silvia to search out partners who could replace Charles, if only for a few hot, sultry minutes while she swayed her hips, sweat dripped from her cheeks, and a flush crept into the soft amber tone of her skin.

Tomás sat at one of the tables that Charles and Silvia had arranged around their backyard. He calculated that the average age of the group at the table was forty, although Charles Compeán had at least ten years on his wife.

His table companions were ambitious, hardworking, and filled with the glow of dreams coming true for them. The overweight jovial woman at the head of the table wore a flowing tropics-inspired batch of cloth that covered her from shoulders to ankles. Flowers and parrots in bright yellows, blues, greens, and reds dotted the material. Tomás thought the outfit made Genevieve Martínez-Higgins look very round. She was a lawyer on her way to becoming the first female Hispanic federal judge from Colorado, if everything fell into place as she had planned. Meanwhile she practiced law at a large downtown firm that specialized in covering the screwups that city and state politicians were bound to commit. Clarke Higgins, her husband, sat to her right, sporting jeans and a sweatshirt that read The Denver Dare—10 K Run for the Children. The race had taken place earlier in the day, and he had worn the complimentary sweatshirt to ward off the hoped-for evening chill. He was an anthropology professor at the University of Colorado, and his specialty—everyone at the party seemed to specialize—was the prehistoric tribes of southwestern Colorado.

The Fernándezes sat on either side of Tomás. They were businesspeople, enterprising folks who had originally invested in a secondhand store in one of Denver's older neighborhoods that gradually had become, with heavy doses of long hours and frantic scrambles for end-of-the-month money, a chic boutique for Mexican folkloric gewgaws, handmade furniture from Central America, and colorful items of clothing from throughout Latin America. From eavesdropping on the group's conversations Tomás learned that Genevieve Martínez-Higgins had bought her exotic dress from Carmen Fernández. She was one of Casa Fernández's best customers. Carmen managed the store, made friends with all the customers, and served as the public face for the business. For six days of the week she lived and breathed the store, and often, more times than she cared to admit, that life flowed over into Sunday. She was a small woman whose face had started to show the creases of her age and work schedule. Reymundo Fernández kept track of the books, ordered inventories, and traveled many weeks during the year, looking for new merchandise. Rey had a quiet, impassive demeanor that implied strength.

The person at the table who most intrigued Tomás had been introduced as Patricia Montelibre. He quickly learned that she taught middle school for the Denver Public Schools. Her contributions to the table talk were serious. She commented on the high dropout rate among the Mexican kids who managed to make it to high school and the depressing numbers of immigrants, legal and illegal, who were going to be denied food stamps because of the latest welfare reform law. When she did laugh, Tomás heard a passionate resonance, and he couldn't help but notice how the soft yellow aura from the Compeáns' kitchen window highlighted the color in her face and the anxious sparkle of her eyes.

He offered to bring her a drink, and she answered, relieved, "Yes, please. I'll take a beer, any kind. It doesn't matter."

When he returned, Patricia was all that remained of the group at the table since the dancing had taken on a sense of lighthearted crisis. The mass hysteria created by the macabre dance that had replaced the macarena as the latest fad had infiltrated the party, by means of a guest who appeared to be the Compeáns' social director. Nearly everyone at the party tried to synchronize their silly gyrations and suggestive hip wiggling in the center of the Compeáns' patio. Many were well past their self-proclaimed limits of alcohol, but the party showed no signs of slowing down.

"Is that Rosemary Rodríguez out there, trying to teach everyone how to dance that crazy thing?"

Tomás recognized the Clerk and Recorder for the City and County of Denver from the many times he had seen her at literary, artistic, and other cultural events. She had been one of the few at a late winter, snow-laden library event where he had talked about his latest book. The dance routine presented another side to the woman who often sat in on meetings at the center of city politics but who also managed a sense of cultural refinement in the stodgy atmosphere of city management. At the moment, desperately coordinating the giddy guests in the arm-shaking and butt-wiggling dance steps, Rodríguez was anything but refined.

"Yes, she's great, isn't she? Silvia likes to have her at her parties. She knows so many people."

"So, how is it that you know Silvia and Charles?"

"I met Silvia at school. We've been friends, off and on, since undergrad. We lived together for a year, almost, at the university. She's like a sister. We've been through a lot together."

His arm moved in an arc that encompassed the backyard. "Then you must recognize everyone here. I can only name a few, and I've hardly even talked to any of these people. You're part of their crowd?"

She shook her head energetically.

"No, not part of the crowd. But I've been around Silvia and Charles enough to know all their friends. Except for you, that is. Silvia mentioned you were coming, of course. She was very flattered. And quite taken with herself that you would show up at one of her parties. She thinks you're famous."

"To tell you the truth, my life hasn't changed that much. I don't think of myself as famous."

She answered, "Mr. Chávez. Señor Chávez, I should say. I have read your books, and your collection of short stories, and even some of the articles you wrote for that Catholic magazine. I know what you do and what you stand for, and I think you should be famous or whatever it is that you want from your writing. There are many things we could talk about from your stories, when you're ready. But not tonight, I guess." Then out of nowhere, or so it seemed to Chávez, she said, "Silvia Compeán wasn't the only person who was impressed with the fact that you would be at her party tonight."

The moment lingered in the cool air. He thought he knew what was happening, and he squeezed every ounce of pleasure out of it that he could, because he also knew that it couldn't continue past that night. The pleasure would last for the remainder of the party and later he would have it to dwell on, to remind him that he was alive.

She handed him a card with her phone number and address and then she said, "When you want to talk again, call me."

He placed the card in his shirt pocket and made a mental note to call his old friend and ask him about the woman. His friend understood these things, he had a knack for ending up in situations with women who were quirky or intellectual or hyperactive or all three at once, but they were always impressive, and they almost always ended up breaking his heart. But Danny Mora never had any regrets.

4

The restaurant on Santa Fe Boulevard once had been only a doorway along the street that opened up to a counter. Short, chatty women had served up a choice of shredded beef, pork *carnitas, chicharrones,* chunks of cow tongue or brains, mixed with rice and green chile, lovingly embraced by giant tortillas, the entire concoction wrapped in aluminum foil, and all for only a dollar. As boys, they had eaten as they walked up and down Santa Fe, grease and chile dripping down their chins and fingers, the hot salsa and the marinated meat taking hold of their taste buds, making them sweat on the coldest day of winter. Those burritos gradually attracted customers from throughout Denver and, as the price of the food increased, the size of the restaurant had correspondingly grown. Carolina's Cocina had become a trendy place, but the food was the same as when

Carolina Aragón herself had loaded up the tortillas. Occasionally Mora and Chávez lamented its popularity, but they often agreed to meet there to talk, and eat, and drink.

Mora and Chávez had no place to return to that they could call the neighborhood where they had grown up, so they relied on these times with each other when they discarded more than thirty years and reverted to "Moony Mora" and "Chacho Chávez," terrors of the West Side, where they were able to set aside the pretensions they exhibited for everyone else. They returned to the place where they treated each other like brothers.

Tomás and Danny both claimed that they didn't remember the origins of the nicknames. When they had to, they explained that they had always called each other those names, and so had their families and friends, their girlfriends. Tomás liked to say, "They just happened. No real reason. Moony was close to Mora, and Chacho was close to Chavez." He knew that made no sense. But Danny would back him up, and then they would steer the conversation to something else.

The truth was that Danny had loved to stare at the moon as a child. When he and Tomás first walked the West Side streets at night as young boys pushing the limits of their parents' rules, Danny stared into the black, smoggy night, searching for the yellow moon. He would say, "It's a crescent." Or, "Almost full." And when Tomás asked him why he cared so much about the moon, what difference it made to anything, Danny would only say, "There's more, that's all. It's not just us, don't you think?" Then he would laugh and push Tomás backward and run, and Chacho would holler, "Asshole! I'm going to kick your ass!" Danny would stop and slowly turn around. "Come on, muchacho. Come on, little boy. Come and get it, 'Chacho!" Then he would run again, with Tomás chasing him, both boys laughing, squealing in the city night, running until they collapsed in a park or against an alley wall, laughing, crying, cursing each other, calling each other "Moony" or "Chacho." They never told anyone that story.

Mora talked about the murdered immigration agent.

"Vigil's killing goes down unofficially as the probable work of Elías Garza, of course, but because Vigil was messing around with Mrs. Garza, not because of the undercover stuff. No one at INS thinks that Vigil's cover was blown. But ironically, that's the part that works on Spann. He wants his friend vindicated. Elías was eventually located in Mexico, where he voluntarily answered the questions of the feds sent to interrogate him. He has more than a hundred witnesses who can prove that he was down there when Vigil was hit. Naturally, he's totally shocked and devastated that his wife's friend has been killed but lets it be known that Vigil hung around with a pretty scary crowd, any one of whom was capable of murder. And Mrs. Garza is saddened too, apparently so much that she takes off for a few weeks to Cancún and an off-shore casino."

Chávez listened with patience, a bit of pity, and anxiety. Periodically he caught himself shaking his head. Daniel Mora was one of a handful of people he knew whose daily job required confronting the violence that all people were capable of but in which only a few, relatively speaking, indulged. The others were police officers and hospital emergency-room staff. In Central America he had known men and women who risked their lives for textbooks for classrooms, but those were different kinds of human beings: they did what was essential and necessary, and when he had been Padre Tomás, he had never felt for those people the same pity or anxiousness that Danny brought out. The heroes were living their lives in the only way they could. Danny simply was earning a buck.

Chávez was puzzled.

"Unofficially, this Vigil is killed by a gangster everyone knows is in the illegal alien and drug smuggling rackets, but he's killed for jumping in bed with the gangster's wife, not because he was about to arrest the gangster? And even that can't be proved? What the hell is the official explanation?"

"It's still an open file. But there are no leads, no loose ends to follow up on. On the other hand, Robert Spann thinks that Elías Garza had uncovered Vigil and knew what he was up to, with Lorraine Garza's treacherous help, and together they set him up and had him killed. Spann wants that ending for his buddy's career, not the ambiguous cloud hanging over it now, not the very large implication that he sacrificed everything for a woman, including his oath to his country, and it cost him his life. Spann wants Vigil remembered as a good agent, not a jerk who carried his brains in his scrotum. He wants him remembered as an agent killed in action. But Spann has very little to support his theory, and so he wants yours truly to come up with something."

Chávez wouldn't try to talk Mora out of taking the job. They had known each other too long for that.

He said, "Spann should think about what he's asking. I don't see what he expects you to do for Vigil or for him. His version could also destroy Vigil's image. If Kiko Vigil was so good at what he did, how could he let himself get trapped by this guy Elías and his wife, unless Vigil really was thinking with his second head, maybe too distracted by Mrs. Garza's feminine attributes? But good God, does anybody really care? That killing happened, what, about six months ago? I barely recall reading about it in the papers. In another six months, no one will remember it at all. What does it matter if Vigil was killed because of his skirt chasing or because of the risks of his job, which I take it he knew and accepted? Is there family or somebody for whom this will make a difference? Anybody?"

Mora turned in the booth and waved at the waitress to bring them another round of drinks.

"Only Robert Spann. Kiko Vigil's last remaining friend in this world, who also happens to be my client."

"It sounds dangerous. Sometimes, Moony, you act like a kid, as though you were playing a role in a movie about somebody else's life, not living your own. When are you going to try something else—"

Mora interrupted him with laughter. "And how about a wife and kids, and a new car or house? Ay, Tomás. Next thing, you'll want to set me up with this new lady friend of yours. Maybe you and Lydia and me and this, what's her name, Patricia, we can double date? Is that what you got in mind for me?"

Chávez looked away. He had told his friend over the phone that he had met a woman at the party, but that was all. His hesitancy and silence gave him away.

Mora smirked, "I get it." He was almost gleeful as the truth sank in.

"Chacho Chávez bumped into a pretty woman that got him to thinking some nasty thoughts, right? The old *pingo* still has life, is that it? *¡Qué bruto!* What a guy! Kiko Vigil was killed for messing around, man! What the hell have we been talking about! You know how Vigil ended up. That will be nothing compared to what Lydia will do to you if she even thought you were thinking about another woman, much less that one flirted with you and got you all into emotional contortions."

"It's not that," Chávez pleaded. "But I guess it is, kind of. She came on to me. At least, I think that's what it was. These days, who knows? Women—they resent it if you ignore them, but they spit on you if you misread them. I guess I've been married too long."

"Yes, man," Mora almost shouted. "You are married, remember? For eight years, if I got the year right when you had that big blowout you called your wedding. Lydia and you were made for each other, if any two people ever were. The fact that you're even talking to me about it proves my point. Any other guy, any other typical guy, I should say, would have picked up this woman, Patricia, bedded her the night of the party, and already have forgotten her name. Here you are, two days later, still agonizing over the fact that she gave you a card with her number on it. It ain't going to happen, Chacho. Just like it never happened with Connie Morelos, back in high school."

He laughed at his repetition of the private joke they had shared since they were teenagers, and Chávez responded in the same way he had for all those years—he slugged Mora on the shoulder and said, "'Chale,' Moony. Me and Connie know what happened that night—I don't care what your cousin said she saw!" Then they both laughed, and their laughter floated through the restaurant as it had for years, and no one else seemed to notice. They laughed as they ate and drank, and soon they were laughing so hard that they almost choked on their burritos. They finished the night laughing and drinking.

Occasionally, in the back of Danny Mora's mind, he wondered how he was going to find out anything new about the murder of Kiko Vigil. Whom should he talk to? Where was the bit of information that would assuage Robert Spann? And at the very back of his mind, so far back that it registered only dimly, he asked, How risky is this job?

When Tomás Chávez stood at the urinal in the men's room of Carolina's Cocina, his thoughts drifted to Patricia Montelibre, and he smiled at his own crassness, his rather disgusting juxtaposition of pissing and memories of the woman. As he walked unsteadily back to Mora and the booth, he remembered the touch of Patricia's hand on his and the insouciant forwardness he had seen in the eyes that had focused on his face. He thought of Lydia, too, and he realized that whatever they had once claimed as their lives together had been lost, without either of them missing that connection. And before he sat down to finish his last drink, he had decided that he should give Patricia a call and discover what those "many things" were that she had wanted to talk about.

■

Silvia Compeán had tried on a dozen different necklaces, but the right one had not yet jumped out at her. A new batch of jewelry from Costa Rica had just arrived at Casa Fernández, and Silvia and Patricia were the first to see the rings, earrings, bracelets, brooches, and neck adornments.

Carmen Fernández definitely was a good friend to have. Silvia offhandedly lifted a gold chain to the light and discovered a pendant made from a bright green, luminous stone. In the middle of the stone an unknown artist had carved the image of a hummingbird, and the light shining through the stone made the bird's wings jump and shimmer, as if the tiny creature had taken flight. Silvia waved at Carmen, who sat smiling behind the cash register.

Silvia chortled. "Carmen! I love it. It's so pretty."

Carmen nodded that she understood that the necklace belonged to Silvia. With her goal accomplished, Silvia returned to the conversation she had been having with Patricia for almost a week, since the night of the party.

"No way, Patty. He's married, he's an ex-priest, and there's just no way."

Patricia groaned. "Stop it, Sil. All I ever said was, Is it a good marriage? That's all. Jeez, you make it sound like I'm some kind of home wrecker or something. I liked the guy as a person, not for a night of wild sex."

"Oh, you're assuming the sex will be wild? You better stop, girl, before this gets out of hand. I know how these things work, how they play out."

Patricia stared at Silvia. "You know how these things work? Is that right? And how is it that you know? What secret affair have you kept from me? And I thought I was your best friend."

"You stop it, Patty. I also know what you're trying to do."

She turned to her friend and whispered to her in the conspiratorial tone she favored when she talked about anything that might be interpreted by others as impolite, much less scandalous.

"He writes interesting books, even if they are a little, uh, vague. I'll admit, he's not bad looking. He's very serious, much more than that playboy lawyer you've been dating. He probably would make a great person to have dinner with, carry on a conversation, get touchy-feely about music and art, and even talk a little politics. Maybe snuggle in front of the fire, drinking brandy."

She paused for dramatic effect.

"If he didn't bring his wife with him, dummy!"

Then she laughed and moved on to Carmen's *calaveras* display. Skeletons seemed appropriate. They helped make her point. Whatever fire had been lit between Patricia Montelibre and Tomás Chávez, Silvia Compeán knew it was her duty to douse it, smother it, kill it dead. She made goals with the idea of meeting them, and there were very few that she failed to reach. Her friend would not be one of the failures.

5

Patricia wasn't above admitting the obvious. She enjoyed sex with Victor Delgado. God knows, she thought, that's not the problem. It was just that so many others also enjoyed it with Victor. She was on the edge of her orgasm, that silvery tightrope that could easily devolve to a gray bottomless well. She was going to miss these sessions. He reached under her and grabbed her ass with both hands and lifted her a few inches off the bed, not for an instant losing his rhythm. Air jumped from his mouth. He appeared to be having a good time. He had that silly smile that had attracted her to him in the first place. She had learned that he wore the same smile whether he was in bed getting his rocks off or sitting on the patio, sipping a Tecate with lime. Oh, that's it, Victor. Go, Victor, go. Almost, baby. Yes, she would miss the sex, the good times, and even his charming, if crude, sense of humor.

And the catty looks from other women who noticed him, not her, when she and Victor arrived anywhere together. They would give her the once-over, and even if she didn't pass the test, there was nothing they could do about it, at least not right then, not right in front of her. He never failed to get a name, a phone number, a look that said it all. She would not miss that. She would not miss Victor's other women. She would not . . . Oh, oh. Ohhh! Thank you, Victor. Not exactly a brain-spasm finish, but it would have to do. Good-bye, Victor. Thanks again, thanks for everything. It's been real.

■

Where to start? Danny Mora tried to answer that question, the same question for each of his cases, early in the morning, when his awakening brain could be fooled into believing that the day held possibilities, that solutions were only a matter of skillful information gathering, meticulous recording of details, and a bit of experienced deduction. Later, after the grind of another day had worn away any trace of optimism, he often understood that he would have to scrounge around for the abundance of luck that so many of his clients' problems required to be solved. It wasn't always enough to be good at the job.

He shifted the gears on his bike to help with the hill on Fifteenth Avenue that started at My Brother's Bar and continued for several blocks up to Zuni Avenue. He had raced the seven and a half miles of the Platte River Parkway south and east from Confluence Park to the beginning of Bear Creek Trail and then leisurely worked his way back to the Highlands neighborhood. No longer a West Sider,

Danny Mora lived in a small and old but comfortable house in one of Denver's well-established neighborhoods that, he confidently believed, would not be bulldozed over and erased. He hadn't loved the projects, the jets, felt no misplaced romanticism about the cheap, ugly buildings that had been his childhood home, but he resented their hostile removal from the city landscape. Maybe a bit of sentiment from the mayor's office—a proclamation or a plaque somewhere—would have helped.

Where to start?

Officially, the cops were out of the equation. Spann had made that much clear. He had already taken the steps that Mora suggested rather than hire a PI—talk with the police, go through their files, walk over the same ground, talk with the same people, and try to come up with something that might have been missed or not completely understood the first time around. Robert Spann had done that and more. He had cajoled, pleaded, and pulled as much rank as he could until he finally spoke with an officer from the Denver police, the agents from within the INS, and the FBI man who had worked the murder. Spann had concluded that they had followed every lead, developed the clues, and tried their damnedest, but no one had come up with a name, not even a face. They all agreed that Elías Garza ordered the death of Kiko Vigil, but the actual triggermen were unknown to those who admitted that they were in the bar that night.

Mora blinked sweat from his eyes and pedaled faster. The dash from the top of the hill to his house had to be a good one, enough of an effort to make him wheeze and grunt. He flew through streets of thirsty elms and withered lawns.

The case had been a natural for the media. What reporter wouldn't jump at the story of the execution of an immigration officer in a bar that catered to noncitizens while it served watered-down liquor and easy access to drugs, sex, and other diversions? The death of the agent had generated a ton of pressure from within the agency, while a reporter for *Westword,* the city's weekly alternative newspaper, had kept the heat on with lurid tales of the shooting and the Tortuga Bar, now closed as a public nuisance. The bar had functioned for years without any official attention other than the usual weekend calls for cops to clear out the drunks or arrest a rowdy homesick mexicano. After Vigil's death, La Tortuga suddenly was the most obvious eyesore along the short stretch of undeveloped Larimer Street.

Mora spread the word that he was looking for any information about the bar or the killing. That word would go to a select few contacts in the police department, and it also would be dropped in other likely locations such as bars, the Mexican bus stations, on the desk of a newspaper reporter who owed Danny a favor. These efforts weren't expected to generate many tangible leads, but at least they would get Danny in the case, and after that beginning he expected to pick up a rhythm that might end somewhere fruitful. They were the motions that had to be gone through by any investigator at the start of a case.

Lorraine Garza had the answers, of course. The women always did. According to Spann, Vigil and Garza had known each other for two years. Vigil's job had been to stop her and her husband's operation, but he had tumbled head over heels into the arms and bed of "Lorraine la Loca."

He hung the bike in his garage, toweled off the sweat,

grabbed a jug of orange juice from the refrigerator, then plopped on the soft chair in his home office. He had converted his patio into a sunroom with large sliding doors. There wasn't much of a view, but across the distant horizon the Rocky Mountains reminded him that the state had beautiful areas—real, honest-to-God nature sanctuaries with pine trees, hordes of insects, and cool, clear streams. From his chair in the middle of the city, with the morning breeze circulating from the open door through the room, Mora eased himself into the mind-set he would need to make headway on Robert Spann's problem. The high from his ride lasted for only a short time, until the morning coolness dissipated and summer's heat slammed the office, but it was enough of what he needed.

He gulped juice and absentmindedly removed his riding clothes for his shower. He stood naked in the glare of the sunshine, exposed to anyone who cared to walk through the alley and peer through the slats of his fence. His long, slender arms and legs were toned and hardened from his bike riding and the exercise regimen he forced on his body at least three times a week. His straight black hair hung over his ears and flopped across his forehead. He was careless about his looks, except for his conviction that he had to present a professional image when he was with clients. He wore well-pressed shirts and colorful ties or sweaters and slacks. No jeans or baseball hats on the job.

He studied copies from Vigil's file. Robert Spann had passed on what he could, without any official approval, and Mora acknowledged that Spann had taken a risk. But that line had been crossed when Spann had hired the detective to look at a case the INS would rather everyone forgot. It was time for that story to die, and it had been quiet for a decent interval. The agency didn't really want to know more about Vigil's involvement with Lorraine Garza. What good could come of that? It would only create more media blather about the incompetence of federal bureaucrats.

The operation had been scuttled, and the agency had to start over. The agency wanted only to wait out the last few convulsions of the dying attention span of the public and hope that no nosy congressional staff person decided to dig a little deeper into the killing of federal agent Francisco Vigil. Other agents would have to bring down the Cardoza-Garza operation. One of these years. After the dust had settled. After another plan had been approved and another team set up. Long after the name of Officer Francisco Vigil had been forgotten. Long after Elías Garza had calmed down, eased his own security, and started doing business as usual again. Too long for Robert Spann.

An option for Mora was to hang out with mexicanos, Guatemalans, and Salvadorans, who would be natural conduits into the society where noncitizens needed people like Elías and Lorraine Garza. For the present at least, he wouldn't try that. Look where Vigil had ended up with that strategy. Mora needed someone else who might have a connection to the Garzas, someone who could inadvertently reveal information that could take him to the next person and, from there, to the next, until he had learned enough to give Spann his best guess. A guess would be all that Spann was going to get from him: his opinion, his version of what went down.

In the nude, his shower on hold, Danny Mora read memos, reports, and court files for an hour before he finally recognized a name that he instinctively assumed would be useful. A court pleading contained the signature and telephone number of the attorney who had represented Elías Garza in one of Garza's numerous interfaces with the U.S. judicial system. Several months had passed since Mora had last visited Victor Delgado, and Delgado might express qualms about talking about his clients—there was that old confidentiality thing—but Danny wasn't worried. Victor Delgado and Danny Mora understood each other quite well. Too well, to Danny's way of thinking. The private investigator would have a conversation with the lawyer, and the lawyer would have no choice but to talk his fool head off and then some. At a minimum, safely ensconced in file cabinets under lock and key, Delgado had to have hard copies of pieces of Garza's life that should never see the revealing glare of day.

And tapes. Delgado's fetish. There had to be tapes.

The lawyer's end of the conversation might end up being nothing more than a grunt and the handing over of a key. In Danny Mora's way of looking at things, that was all he needed. That was how he made his living. He had conversations with people.

■

Tomás stared at Lydia and had to give her credit. After all the arguments, the broken promises, the digs at each other—after all the years—he still thought she was an attractive woman. Her soft brown hair and sexy legs could produce a second look from most men as easily now as they had when Tomás had worked that second look into a date and then a relationship and eventually a marriage that, for the most part, had worked. At least he had always said that to himself, and others, if they asked. His marriage worked, his writing was a critical success; in short, his life meant something. Tomás wanted very much for his life to work out. He had no time for failure, in his art or his marriage.

He had moved past the guilt over what his mother had called his disloyalty to the church. She didn't try to understand his explanations for leaving the priesthood, although she demanded to hear them over and over. It had been impossible to articulate a coherent explanation for turning his back on what had been his and his mother's dream for years, but, when he thought about it, certainly no more difficult than it had been when his childhood friends, Danny Mora included, had demanded to hear why it made sense to become a priest in the first place. His mother rejected his rationalizations and, fundamentally, him, too. Her communications with him since that dark day when he showed up at her house unannounced, a battered suitcase his only possession, had been curt and often pernicious. She hadn't attended his wedding, but, with a bit of calculating irony that Tomás appreciated, she had grown close to Lydia. Tomás accepted his Catholic Mexican mother's rigidity, but he refused to conclude that it meant he had failed at something. He had moved on, he told himself, that's all.

He saw that it was happening again. The beginning of what looked like the last chapter of a part of his life that he didn't want to do anymore—the beginning of the end of his marriage.

The argument had started as they all had lately. Questions about money—why had she spent so much on such frivolous things? He had already forgotten what it was that she had brought home in the shopping bags. Then the real questions popped up, questions that implicated trust and confidence and other vague notions of compatibility that Lydia insisted on throwing at him and against which he had no retort.

His own father had left the house when Tomás was ten. It had occurred during a series of long, drawn-out arguments that Tomás blamed on his mother. He didn't begrudge his father's departure, didn't even think he had done anything wrong. Just the opposite. The boy Chacho and then the man Tomás envied the father for resolving a situation that had been intolerable. The heat and vicious-ness of the words that Lydia and Tomás threw at each other brought back the memories of his parents' arguments that he thought he had laid to rest long ago. Tomás felt himself melting into the image he had of his father just before he left the house—angry, tight-lipped, and impotent before the furious woman who demanded so much and gave back so little in return.

Lydia Chávez rarely shouted at her husband. She wanted to reason with him, to make her point and make him agree because Tomás never said anything that turned her thinking. When she had loved him, it had been easy to let it go, to compromise herself and slough off the prin-ciple that had energized her in the battle. But now, she gave no quarter and expected none. She would push to the brink or be pushed into it.

"You're not making sense, Tomás," she said, knowing that accusations of lack of clarity were the perfect bait to make him rise to the hook. Tomás hated above all to be unclear, although you wouldn't know it from his writing. She grinned, and he couldn't take it.

He sputtered, "I can't help it if you can't understand! You're the one not making sense, the one who insists that we have no partnership!"

Lydia smiled inwardly. He made it too easy.

"Partnership? Is that what we have? I thought we were married, not in business together. That's just like you, to reduce our personal issues to dry, economic terms."

She was in command. But it wasn't enough. She pulled the strings and orchestrated the dance, but she was ready to cry because she knew what she was doing, and she didn't want to hurt him, she wanted them to quit the fight, to hold each other and ease each other through the night, but she couldn't stop, she couldn't hold back, and she knew, too, that it was over for them.

"Damn you, Lydia! Quit talking gibberish! This is about us. Don't you care what the hell is happening here? Don't you care?"

He sat down and dropped his head in his hands. Low groans came from his throat.

Lydia smothered her whimpers in her own hands. She thought about screaming at him, about trying to force into his brain, if not his heart, the truth that she knew and that he had to recognize—they needed each other, they had to have each other to preserve love, to stay alive. She couldn't do it. She had no more shouts in her, and very few tears. The words were long used up. She walked out of the room, not looking back at the man whom she didn't know anymore, accepting that what she felt for him had changed, and lessened.

He left that night. He didn't tell her where he was going, although she silently pleaded with him to quit acting like a crazy man. He didn't call his mother, but he had no doubt that Lydia would, and that the two of them would agree it was better he had left. He did call Danny Mora and left a message that he would call again when he knew what the hell he was doing. He couldn't guess when that would be.

"A moment of your time, *querida*. We should talk. This is not good for either one of us. We have to get on with business. If I am willing to let this unseemly episode slip away, into the night where it belongs, then why can't you? Even if you are finished with me, we still have to get on with our lives, and that means paying the bills, no? You and I together, as always. That is the only way this will work."

Elías Garza spoke softly to his wife. The time for more physical exhortations and displays should have passed. It had been necessary, but he hadn't enjoyed it, and now all he wanted was to return to a semblance of what they once had, before the Vigil messiness. She had learned her lesson, of that he was positive, but this incessant silence, this refusal to cooperate with him, to get back to work—it was all just female stubbornness.

If anyone should be holding a grudge, it should be me, not Lorraine. I am the cuckold, no? I am the man my employees talk about behind my back, no? I am the one running the risk of losing everything that old man Cardoza had entrusted to me, and for what? A woman who will not even talk to me? No! It will stop once and for all, tonight.

She watched him approach, calm and self-assured. She forced herself to reflect the same calm and self-assurance. *The bastard had better stay away.* She clutched a rhinestone-specked purse. She would not endure more beatings or humiliation in front of their old friends—friends, ha! His fat *rateros* and their ugly *putas*. She could see what they thought of her in their eyes, and in their smiles and nervous giggles when they were privy to his wrath. That blue-eyed fake blonde from Veracruz had revealed as much last night when the tequila and cocaine had overwhelmed the bitch's common sense.

"Sweetie, you've lorded over the rest of us just because the boss has been hypnotized by your *panocha*. Those days are over."

Lorraine had tossed the blonde on her fat ass and cleared the house of everyone.

Elías reached for her arm.

She screeched, "Stay away from me. I won't take any more from you. This is it. I don't care what you do. I don't care anymore."

She slipped her hand inside the purse.

Elías stood over her as she sat in the chair. He couldn't believe his ears. What a woman!

She was nervous, but on guard. If needed, she could whip out the weapon and fire it before he—

He kicked and his shoe slammed her jaw. Her neck twisted and the chair fell back from the force of the blow. Flecks of blood sprayed the wall. Her purse flew to the corner of the room. A small pistol dropped on the floor.

On the first level of the huge house, the servants heard the crash. Some retreated to their rooms, while others scurried to the garage, where they smoked cigarettes and drank beer. The boss would be occupied for a while.

Elías Garza straddled his semiconscious wife's body. He ripped the blouse from her torso and scratched her skin as he pinched and pulled her flesh. He lifted her and tore off her remaining clothes. She was naked under him, bleeding, dazed, and babbling about Kiko Vigil. He slapped her face, again and again, until his palm ached. Then he unzipped his pants and took from his wife what she had been withholding since the death of her lover. He continued to hit her. She begged, not for herself but for Kiko's life. He screamed at the top of his lungs, drowning out the whimpers of Lorraine. The men in the garage heard him, and some made the sign of the cross.

"The devil has come to this house," one whispered.

Another man laughed and responded, "The devil has lived here for years. Tonight La Loca gets what she deserves."

Several of the men nodded in agreement. They were able to drink several beers each and smoke many packs of cigarettes before they were summoned to clean up the mess in the bedroom.

7

Silvia had insisted on trooping to Cherry Creek to a chichi new place in the mall that only a woman with money and the right attitude would consider for lunch.

She had told Patricia, "We can indulge ourselves, and why not? We're not barbarians. We have as much right as any white, rich, fat old lady to sit in Cherry Creek and pamper ourselves with those exquisite little tarts."

Patricia's reasons for agreeing to the lunch were less obvious but just as self-indulgent. A week had passed since she had informed Victor Delgado that their last "date" had been, really, the last one, *la ultima vez,* as the songs say. Surely someone was talking about her. And where was Tomás Chávez keeping himself?

Patricia loved Sil like any sister should. They had scrimped and sacrificed in school. She remembered days of living on popcorn and the times when they were saved by accepting dinner dates with frat rats who then had to be fought off the rest of the night. Silvia had bagged a rich man, so why shouldn't she enjoy it? After all, they weren't barbarians.

"Silvia, are you going to tell me or what? What's happened to Tomás Chávez? It's all over town that he left his wife, or she threw him out, depending on who's talking. Now what? How serious is it? Where is he?"

Silvia rolled her eyes.

"La Patty has no shame. The body of the Chávez marriage is still warm, and you want to cover it with dirt and hop on poor Tomás's bones before he knows what hit him. How crass, girl. It hasn't been that long since you and Victor Delgado were a major item. How quickly the fickle hearted can turn."

Silvia spoke only half in jest. She was worried that her friend was intent on setting herself up for the big hurt. Tomás Chávez was a no-hoper if there ever was one.

Patricia teased, "You must not know anything."

"Patty, there's nothing worse than fooling around with a married man, unless it's fooling around with a married man on the rebound," Silvia responded defensively. "From what I know about Lydia and Tomás Chávez, they'll be back together before you can say, 'My place or yours?' If I were you, I'd steer clear of that messy domestic situation for about ten years. After that, if they're still separated, maybe then you can look him up. He's an ex-priest, for pity's sake! How dull can that be?"

Patricia smiled at Silvia's clumsy attempts to protect her. Silvia couldn't resist the deep-seated need to spill her guts that all *habladoras*, gossips, shared. Any news, dirt, or rumor about Tomás Chávez wouldn't have been safe with Silvia. Silvia practiced the religious tenet of spreading the word. In her case it meant revealing any secret entrusted to her to anyone who might join her for lunch. Her continued reluctance to lay out anything of substance about Tomás could mean only that she was without a clue. Patricia would have to try something else.

An easy explanation for her behavior didn't exist. Comparing Tomás and Victor was an exercise in surrealism. The two were so different it was as though they lived on separate planets. She had crossed the space between the two, yet there was no logical connection between Tomás and Victor, no simple way to diagram a natural progression from the flashy, good-times attorney to the introverted, very mental writer. She hadn't known Tomás for any length of time, but she had to admit she was interested, just like she had accepted that she would be one of Victor's notches on his well-oiled gun the first time they had danced together. Oh, well, she thought, don't analyze it, enjoy it. Maybe she was maturing in her tastes. Maybe her attraction to Tomás signaled a new level of relationship for her. As long as the wife stayed out of the picture.

Danny Mora had oatmeal, coffee, and a newspaper at the
Tecolote Café, only a few blocks from his house. He walked
to the café when he needed a break from the cold cereal
that he invariably fixed for himself. The place had been in
the neighborhood for years, under several different own-
ers, and he hadn't been a regular until the latest change.
Clorinda and Eufemio Espinoza were an older couple who
preferred speaking in Spanish but could communicate in
at least two other languages.

"*Viajamos mucho.* We travel a lot," they had once
explained to Danny.

In their physical appearances the Espinozas reminded
Danny of his parents, and since the food was decent and
the prices cheap, he made the Tecolote Café part of his
weekly routine. His parents had been dead for years, and

the small restaurant was as close as he could get to anything that recalled his family.

Over his last cup of coffee, he thought about his upcoming meeting with Delgado.

It was a risk, of course. Delgado might get squeamish and decide that Mora had gone too far. Or maybe he didn't care about Danny Mora and ancient history. Danny Mora had worked for Victor Delgado on a number of cases in a history of employment that eventually both had come to regret. And there was no guarantee that Delgado had anything Mora could use. He was trying to get a hook on the Vigil killing that dozens of experienced lawmen had somehow missed. The chances were slim to none that he would succeed, but it meant that he had to go where the others hadn't been. Delgado could be a dead end and a waste of time. But Mora calculated that there were a finite number of situations where people had shared secrets with Elías Garza that could hurt the man—in meetings with Don Geronimo Cardoza, his boss and partner in crime, and certainly not a possible source for Mora; in intimate settings with Lorraine Garza, the wife, currently vanished from public view; and in trial preparation conferences with any one of a dozen defense attorneys, in the States and Mexico, who had kept Garza out of a federal pen. Victor Delgado was one of those attorneys.

Delgado usually didn't do such high-stakes defense work, and the odds among Delgado's competition had favored him falling on his face and most likely ending up in a hole in the mountains dug by the gangster's embittered henchmen. But Victor did have a good reputation for the ability to elegantly tap-dance his way through pretrial motions and procedural arguments, greatly expanding the meaning of the phrase "speedy trial."

Garza had come to Victor Delgado by way of his old law school chum Jorge Candelaria, a quite successful, overpriced attorney in Los Angeles who had a base of international clients from the Philippines to Peru. Jorge did his buddy a favor, and it had fallen into place for Victor. He stalled and delayed the Denver court long enough for Elías's California team of attorneys to work out an arrangement with the Los Angeles U.S. Attorney's office, and the next thing everyone knew, the Colorado charges were dropped and Garza's hand was slapped by a California judge. The favorable fallout for Victor had meant a higher profile among his colleagues, several new clients, and a weekend with a pair of women sent to him by Garza as a token of appreciation. Garza had picked up on Victor's favorite hobby.

All that had been last year's news, and Delgado's situation had returned to about normal for him.

Mora left the restaurant and briskly walked to his home. He looked over a few notes he had made from his interview with Spann, made sure all the locks were secured, and then drove to Delgado's office near the courthouse.

Mora didn't recognize the woman who asked him to have a seat in the reception area. Victor Delgado went through receptionists like other attorneys used up legal pads. Mora waited. Twenty minutes ticked away.

The morning had been warm, bright, and oppressive, and Mora at least was grateful for Delgado's air-conditioning.

The receptionist appeared and showed him to the conference room.

Mora sat at an oval table and waited again. Ten minutes

passed. The conference room also served as the office library, and the walls were covered with shelves of case reporters, overflowing loose-leaf binders, and statutes. A lone empty ashtray sat on the table. A blinking computer with a tray of CDs lying next to it rested on a small desk in the corner. The words *Victor Delgado, Esq.* moved across the computer screen, lime green letters against a black background.

Delgado finally walked in the room. He stared at Danny Mora. He was a tall, angular man who peered from behind wire-rimmed glasses. Because he had no need to make a good first impression on Mora, he wore no coat, but his slacks and shirt appeared to be fresh out of the Neiman Marcus box. A pair of leather suspenders and a brilliant blue bow tie, splashed with nervous streaks of yellow, finished off the package. Victor habitually wore his shit-eating grin like one of his florid ties, part of his outfit, essential to his costume. He wasn't smiling as he acknowledged Daniel Mora.

"Moony Mora. I guess I can't say I'm happy to see you. I'm surprised that you're even here. I don't need an investigator; I have a very good one now. What do you want?"

The lawyer lit a cigarette and leaned against one of the bookshelves.

Danny said, "We both know what each of us thinks about the other one. I wouldn't be here except that I have a job that requires me to talk with you. So, I won't waste your or my time."

Delgado smirked. He flicked ashes in the ashtray. He waited for Mora to continue.

"You once represented Elías Garza. I want to see the files for that case. All the files, including your notes of interviews with his wife and anyone else."

He paused. Delgado's eyes twitched, and his fingers played with his glowing cigarette.

"The tapes, too. All of them. I'll take them with me and send them back when I'm finished. It shouldn't take me more than a couple of days."

Delgado reached for the pack of cigarettes in his shirt pocket and almost burned himself with the one smoking in his hand.

"Get the hell out!"

He turned to leave. Danny Mora jumped to his feet and grabbed the taller man by the shoulder. He whirled him around.

"Cut the melodrama, Victor. You'll give me what I want, and you'll do it now."

They stared at each other. Tiny drops of perspiration appeared on the forehead of the lawyer. He stood at least a head taller than Mora, but he made no move to remove the hand from his shoulder.

This is crazy. I went to law school for this bullshit! Mora's way out of his league if he's digging into Garza's business. And it will be my ass if Garza knows I even talked with this maniac.

The thoughts were coming fast and furiously, at a pace that Victor had a hard time sustaining.

How far will Mora go? I should have taken care of him long ago, back when the Compeán mess first got out of hand.

He sucked in a deep pull of cigarette smoke and expelled it with a rush in the direction of Mora's face. He silently counted to three, took another puff, then squeaked out the words.

"It's your funeral, asshole. Marie will get what you want. And if Garza asks, I'll tell him you stole the stuff from me.

Don't show your face around here again. You're cashed in, Mora. Don't pull any more crap. Even I got limits."

He jerked his shoulder from Mora's hand, jammed the cigarette into the ashtray, and left the room.

Daniel Mora, private investigator, man of reasonable expectations, thought it had worked out well, much easier than he had anticipated.

■

The room felt like an oven. Billy Cordero sweated rivers in the strict confines of his chair. He had a tape of classic rhythm and blues blasting through his headphones, but he wasn't playing his instrument. His heart wasn't in it.

"Candy, Candy, Candy. I call my sugar Candy. He's gonna be just dandy."

He sang along with Big Maybelle to himself, but even in his imagination he was no match for the magnificent, resonant voice that broke into sensuous squeaks at all the right places. In his present mood, it took no rocket scientist to predict how badly he would butcher the tune with his saxophone. His disgust at his situation had affected his music. He had lost his chops. His dreams had come back, and that bozo who had broken in hadn't helped his state of mind. He had to face up to it. He had nurtured great expectations about his move to the city, he had those old high hopes. But truth be told, Denver hadn't panned out for Billy.

First, the so-called job at the senior center fell through—too much red tape was the only explanation he had been given for not lasting out the week. Red tape for what? Then the break-in and consequent need to talk to the herd of cops that willy-nilly paraded through his two rooms. They had been more interested in checking him out than in looking for the thief. Questions about his source of income, his previous addresses, his plans for the future, his proposed length of stay in the Mile High City—all the usual crap. No wonder he felt burned out.

The cops hadn't been that inquisitive the night of the shooting. The break-in had been the final straw, but that damn shooting should have clued Billy that he wasn't meant for any Rocky Mountain High. That night, the shooting night, the cops had pretty much treated him with contempt and demanded that he "get out of the way!" as they had so professionally expressed it. One of them had taken a few notes, but no one ever got back to him after that. Only his pal, his business partner, David the Dancer, had listened completely and intently to all of his story, and David had been duly impressed, but that was David, and, honestly, what in the hell was David going to do about it? David had been there with him that night anyway. He knew the goddamned story before Billy told it to him. Billy had done his duty, fulfilled his civic responsibility, and what had it gotten him? Nothing, nada, nyet.

Screw it. He wanted to forget all that had happened outside that wetback bar downtown, that night after the long afternoon when he and David had done their dog-and-pony show for the baseball fans. They had made a good chunk of change from his playing and David's playing around, and they had toured Larimer, spending their take on beer. Not in the wetback bar, no way in that bar, where, with David's strangeness and Billy's wheelchair, they would have been tossed out on their asses. In the other bars, the sports joints, where the bartenders were more tolerant, for at least one beer anyway.

When they were down to their last two bucks they walked Larimer, searching for something. The tourists were long gone, and the street was nearly empty and silent. They had decided they were trying to find a way home, hoping to catch a ride from someone, anyone, when they heard the sharp explosions from the bar. The slash of light that had pointed the way, the light that had shone on the street from within the bar, went dark. Men and women ran from the bar, screaming and shouting in Spanish, tumbling against Billy and David. A man lugging a squirming package across his shoulders ran from the doorway and over Billy, who lost control of his chair. The old fear had grabbed Billy. He crashed his chair on the curb and tumbled to the street. David ducked behind a car, waiting for Billy to tell him what to do. Billy couldn't help David. He lay on the street, half drunk, dazed, and not sure if he was back in Nam or still on the street. He was a tiny, quivering animal, clutching his instrument to his chest, immobile and totally freaked.

The man looked up and down the street, then hurriedly ran to a car parked only a few yards from where Billy lay huddled. The man pulled and pushed a bundle, and as Billy watched, it came to him that the bundle was a woman with long hair. The man held his hand over the woman's mouth as she vainly jerked and squirmed, trying to free herself from the man's grip. The rear passenger door opened, and the man hit the woman on the side of the head with his fist. Billy flinched. The woman went limp, and the man dumped her in the car. The car drove away, but Billy knew what he had seen—the face of the man who had slugged the woman.

When the man punched the woman, the rubber bands holding his mask to his head had snapped and the mask fell away. The mask was a cheap ninety-nine-cent thing you could buy in any *miscelánea* shop, a half-face thing with a silly grin and a big nose, and it was the only mistake the man made that night.

He might forget a few things in his life, hell, he had forgotten a lot of things in his life, but Billy would never forget that face. He told David, "Don't ever get hit by that guy." David had solemnly nodded, then Billy had described that face as the face of a man possessed and David had said, "You mean like the devil?" Billy looked at him as though it was the first time he had seen David's large head and thinning hair. Sometimes David was too smart for his own good.

Billy wished he hadn't seen that face.

After the car sped into the night, Billy had called out to David.

"Help me up, David. Get me in the chair."

The frightened, whimpering David did what he could, and by the time the cops arrived, David and Billy were just another pair of gawking spectators lost in the jostle of onlookers who gathered in the first hour of the new day because a man had been shot, and who could sleep anyway with all the sirens? A rookie cop was given the job of checking out the crowd. He eyed the pair and assumed that they were come-latelies to the scene. Before the cop could ask a question, Billy told him that they had been outside the bar when the shots had been fired. The policeman took that statement to mean that Billy and David hadn't seen anything of importance that related to what had happened inside the bar. The cop made a note of it, asked for their names, and

Billy said, "Frankie Johns," but when David had trouble spitting out any words, forget a name, the officer walked away, disgusted, mumbling something about "wasting time with a couple of damn bums." Billy Cordero didn't tell the policeman about the face that he would never forget.

Damn, it's hot, he thought. He wiped sweat from his face with the back of his sleeve.

Nope, Denver wasn't the end of the rainbow for Billy Cordero. Nothing had come together. No job in sight, no way to get ready for next month's rent for Mrs. Vega. He hadn't heard of any reward or anything like that in the wetback bar shooting. There was talk on the street about some kind of investigator who was asking around about that shooting, but that meant nothing to Billy. No one wanted to hear from Billy.

He looked at the money on the desk. He had enough for a bus ticket to Albuquerque, and if he hustled and didn't eat much, he could make it to San Antonio before the fall, which in Colorado could mean snow. He didn't like snow. He'd heard a lot about San Antone, or San Anto, as his father would have called it. Good-looking city, good-looking *tejanas* and old-fashioned *conjunto* music—his kind of place. Yes, Billy let himself get excited about the change. Start over, try again. That's all he ever had going for him anyway.

He stopped tripping for a sec. He didn't want to leave David. The guy had come to depend on him, and their act was good, as long as David didn't get carried away. Billy had to keep a leash on the guy, or he would be off—zoom, into the stratosphere. Hell, why not ask him to go? Silly-ass street-flower-selling jobs were everywhere, even Texas. Sure, why not ask David to come along? Billy had always traveled alone, he didn't want to have to depend on any-one for anything, that was where most crips went wrong, but David had proved to be a decent guy, a good friend. The trip would be like a payoff for hanging in there with old Frankie Johns, whose luck never seemed to turn for the better. Tomorrow he would talk David into packing a bag, and they would be off to the land of the Alamo and yellow roses. To hell with Denver and midnight shootings and ill-mannered cops!

He felt better already. He raised the saxophone to his lips and started to play. The sweet, cool notes dissipated the heat, separating it like a speeding boat splits the water, and he knew that it would be all right. Pedestrians heard the music float from his room and marveled that someone could be enjoying himself in such heat.

David the Dancer, dispirited all day because of the lack of business, perked up at the sounds of his friend's instru-ment. He launched the latest steps of the Dance of the Flower Seller. The music always had that effect. That guy, Billy or Frankie or whatever the hell, that guy. It was all David the Dancer could say, but it was enough.

Billy Cordero, who called himself Frankie, was back!

A television set glowed in the sunken den, but there was no sound, and the screen flickered to an empty couch. The southwestern decor impressed no one. A futuristic-looking stereo system hung on the wall and repeatedly played a homemade CD of do-wop odes to teenage love and Mexican ballads about hopeless love.

In the kitchen there were signs of life, however limited. Two drunk men sat at opposite ends of a built-in table covered with Mexican tile. They talked about life or work or marriage or children. No one listened.

Reymundo Fernández mumbled, "Carmen's naggin' again about the vacation. I'm sick and tired of hearin' about that *pinche* vacation! I don' have no time or money for a vacation. A trip to one of the resorts where she can get back her tan and prowl the *mercados* could cost thousands of pinche dollars!"

His head dropped an inch closer to his chest.

He continued mumbling. "I've told her, a hunnerd times. I can get any piece of junk from Mexico that she wants, wholesale! That ain't good enough! She wants to get away from the city, to use up time doing nothin' and bring back dozens of bags of pinche clothes. Trinkets! Damn dust collectors! What the hell do I want to do that for? I travel nine months of the year as it is!"

Clarke nodded, although he wasn't sure what he had heard. At another time he would have noted, and emphasized, that Carmen and Rey Fernández had to work hard. Carmen spent days on the accounts, double checking the books and carefully, almost obsessively filling in all the forms that the various levels of government demanded. And he would have nodded in agreement when Rey described how he had to travel for weeks, humping from one village to another, eating bad food, traveling over roads that were built for goats, haggling over prices and quantities with regional jefes, and all the time not sure if anybody in those mosquito-infested dumps ever understood one damn word.

Fernández finished his point. "I'm tellin' you, Clarke. Satisfyin' the fashion whims of the spoiled *viejas* of this city who got extra money to piss away is not as easy as it sounds!"

Rey had drunk pitchers of Clarke Higgins's famous tequila sunrises for more than two hours, and as the night aged, the ratio of tequila to grenadine and orange juice had drastically tipped in favor of the alcohol. Rey couldn't be blamed for spouting off in so reckless a fashion. If he had considered his words before he belched them in Clarke's face, he wouldn't have uttered them, or at least he would have followed them with an advisory such as "present company excluded," although, at present, there was no one who remotely resembled a spoiled vieja in the room.

However, earlier in the evening, Genevieve Martínez-Higgins had sported at least three pieces of jewelry from his store and a purple-and-teal variant of her ever present peasant dress, her favorite article of clothing from Casa Fernández. It was no secret that Genevieve had a good deal of extra money, although her husband didn't necessarily think that she pissed it away.

Rey had said something that required Clarke to respond, but exactly why wasn't clear to him at that precise moment.

He managed to say, "You love your work—don't shit me! All these women that buy your stuff! They keep you and little Carmen in that big house and those fancy cars. Come on, Rey. Cut the crap!"

"It ain't crap. We been livin' on the edge for so long that the pinche bank can't believe we didn't fold up last year. Tough fuckin' year. We were on the verge of bankruptcy, of closin' the store and havin' to start all over. We ain't got nothin' to fall back on. Nothin'! Thank God, we pulled out of it, no thanks to your president. NAFTA, my ass! I got screwed, man. Cheap Mexican goods flooded the border towns, and anyone from up here in the north can pick up the same stuff we got in our store for half the price we had to pay for it just a few months ago! That's what I get for voting for that pinche white guy! Carmen insisted; I knew it was a mistake. What the hell does she know about politics!

I think she just thought he was good-lookin'. What a reason to vote for a person! Guy gets the women's panties all wet and he gets to be president. What a country!"

Finally the conversation had turned to a subject that Higgins felt secure spouting off about. He took a slow drink from his empty glass while he decided what he should clarify for Mr. Fernández: NAFTA, the voting trends of middle-class U.S. Hispanics at the beginning of the new century, or the real reasons voters cast their votes for particular candidates? He was about to say something about middle-aged women voters and their proclivity to attach themselves to candidates who resembled John Kennedy or, more likely, Robert Redford, when he noticed that Rey Fernández had collapsed in his chair. He looked dead. Higgins was trying to focus on the steps he should take to call for help when a quick snort flapped Fernández's lips. The professor heaved a heavy sigh of relief. Dead men don't snore.

He stood up, wobbled against the table, and said, "S'cuse me, Rey. I think I'll go on up to bed. Uh, you can stay here if you like. What you think happened to Carmen and Gen?"

When he didn't get an answer, he zigzagged up the stairs, bounced against the wall, and twice fell to one knee.

His wife lay on the bed in a pair of cotton pajama bottoms and a loose-fitting T-shirt. Genevieve had stretched out on the sheet without blankets. She wasn't asleep. He grunted at her and wiggled out of his clothes. When he plopped on the bed next to Genevieve, he said, "Rey's out, downstairs. Where's Carmen? She ought to take him home. I don't think he can drive."

"I took her home hours ago. You're a real bastard,

58   •

Clarke. You get drunk with Rey and don't remember a damn thing. Why do you have to act like a kid when he's around? He's a drunk. Is that what you want to be?"

She rolled on her side, away from him. He wanted to tell her that she had it wrong. He couldn't form the words. The bed started spinning. The next few minutes were crucial. He either passed out or threw up. He would have to make a run for the bathroom if he felt his guts squeeze into his throat. He waited for sleep or his guts.

"Every damn time. Rey starts in on his sob story about growing up in the barrio, on the wrong side of the tracks in Albuquerque, and you try to top him with your stupid stories about your alcoholic father and your poor, dead mother. Then he brings up the so-called gang he was in and the time he spent in jail, and you wail about running away from home, the army. But you don't stop. You spill out drivel about the dormitory, after you patched things up with your father and you went back to school, as if Rey cared. You're a white man, Clarke. Live with it. You can't ever be an oppressed Chicano, no matter who you drink with, no matter who you marry."

He squirmed and tried to put his arm around her shoulders. He could only get as far as her elbow. He rubbed her elbow and mumbled something that neither of them could decipher.

She jerked her arm away from him.

"Fuck you, Clarke."

He passed out.

10

Daniel Mora's customarily neat office had undergone an unexpected mutation in the several days since he had taken on the Kiko Vigil case. The investigation had turned out to be paper-intensive. In one corner lay the scattered files that Robert Spann had provided. Numerous pages from the files were marked with yellow Post-its, and several of those pages had passages marked with yellow highlighter. Mora had smeared the yellow ink over words, sentences, and paragraphs as he read them, often because of no more than an uncomfortable feeling the entry produced in his belly. He had learned long ago to go with his gut, to trust the sensations and vibrations that he picked up from people, places, or situations.

A wooden rectangular table abutted the back wall of the office across from some of the masks he had recovered from

Mexico. The heavy, cumbersome piece of furniture had a dark, thick grain and a rustic design and it looked ancient. Víctor Delgado's box of documents on Elías Garza perched in the center of the table. Around the box, covering the richness of the art of the handmade table, Mora had strewn several sheets of paper and more than a dozen cassette tapes.

Mora had retrieved the table from his grandfather's house in the New Mexican village where the old man had lived for most of his eighty-seven years. After his *abuelo*'s death, Daniel had been informed by a somber aunt that he could have the table. The old man had wanted him to use it for his "paperwork."

The old table had deep indentations, permanent stains, and a smell that could change from morning to night. A whiff of pine might greet a client, or a gust of smoky air, or the scent of red earth dampened by an evening rainstorm. He was accustomed to people sniffing and looking around the office for a burning stick of incense or a perfumed candle. The table kept Danny in touch with his mother's side of the family, many of whom still lived in mountain villages of northern New Mexico.

He heard the movement of the wall clock's arms as the minutes ticked away. Twelve-thirty, half past midnight. For the fourth time that week he had listened to portions of the tapes and pored over the documents from Spann and Delgado, looking for anything that would ignite a flicker of understanding. There hadn't been much.

The tapes were typical Delgado. The attorney had recorders hidden all over his office. They captured his interviews, conversations, and arguments with clients and witnesses. Mora assumed that his discussion with Víctor Delgado in the office library also had been preserved on tape. He didn't give it a second thought. Mora had listened to graphic and outrageous details of Garza's criminal activities. Although ostensibly secure because of the attorney-client relationship, the information on the tapes could end Garza's world if heard by the wrong pair of ears. Mora cringed as Garza and Delgado joked and laughed about kidnappings, beatings, torture, and murders. Victor's pleasure over his introduction to the "inside" of high-level criminality permeated the tapes, as did Garza's obvious enjoyment in retelling the stories and his pride in his accomplishments. The man used excellent English to boast. But, Mora had to conclude, although the tapes were damaging to Garza for several different reasons, they added nothing about Kiko Vigil. Garza might want the tapes, but Mora had no use for them.

And it was unlikely that he could do anything with the background information on Vigil that Spann had gathered. Family, friends, enemies, coworkers, and men he had arrested or had sent back to their native countries had all been checked out by the Denver police and the feds. Kiko Vigil had enough baggage from his job and his love affairs that a dozen suspects easily could be singled out for special attention, and that was what had happened. Several people had been the recipients of repeated and prolonged visits from the different law enforcement agencies that had worked the case. Nothing had panned out. The connection to Garza could be in that group, and maybe digging deeper among them was called for, but Mora felt certain that the link wouldn't be exposed that easily.

Kiko's personal papers included several newspaper articles in a file folder labeled "research." These articles were pasted on thin cardboard and marked with the date and source. There were the usual stories about the border patrol, some planted by the agency to boost flagging morale or improve the public image, and other so-called investigative pieces whose headlines claimed to reveal the whole truth about the illegal immigrant situation in the United States. Mora smiled at that. Illegal Immigrant Situation.

A few articles about the tragedies of the smuggling business surprised Mora. Robbery, murder, rape, and torture were often included in the price for entering the country. The details in the stories made Mora wince. Some of the people who wanted a taste of the American dream were so helpless and at the mercy of the worst brand of thugs that he asked himself why anyone would risk the trip. He answered with a quick glance around his comfortable office. How much risk is too much for a chance to escape hunger?

One story looked particularly dog-eared, although it lacked the cardboard backing of the other pieces. It was a straightforward news item about the discovery of four bodies buried in the Arizona desert. The local sheriff speculated that they were drug runners who had battled a rival gang or illegals who had met up with the wrong kind of welcoming committee in their new country.

The article included a quote from the sheriff. *"We find bodies out there every so often. These people kill each other on a regular basis. There's probably a dozen more out there that one day a wild dog will dig up. It's impossible to get to the bottom of any of these killings. Most times, nobody even knows who these people are."*

The story finished with the speculation that the victims

were two males and two females, and the remains of at least two of the victims appeared to be those of children.

He moved his scrutiny to information about the night of Vigil's killing. Danny Mora had been bothered by the lack of clean information that had been gathered from the scene. Several descriptions of the shooter reflected the witnesses' panic when they saw the gun or heard the first shots. There had been at least one man, most likely two, most agreed on that, although a bartender swore he saw three men enter the bar seconds before the guns exploded and the lights went out. The men were described as Hispanics, probably Mexican, one average height, one a bit shorter, each wearing a blue baseball cap, no logos, and dressed in jeans and dark shirts. Or they could have been African Americans, tall and muscular, dressed in suits. Or . . .

That was it. Nothing about their faces, length of hair, shoes, whether they said anything to Vigil before they shot him, nothing about the way they left the scene with Lorraine Garza bundled up and secure. Everyone in the bar had been too scared or too drunk to give any more detail.

Mora listed the people the police talked to the night of the shooting. Fifty-eight names stared at him, in alphabetical order. He concentrated on those who had been on the street, after the killing, but their statements added nothing of substance to the vague narratives of the bar's customers. The outsiders, as Mora mentally labeled those who hadn't been in the bar at the time of the shooting, had heard the shots, the sirens, and then had converged on the scene out of common morbid curiosity. The customers had rushed out of the bar and run for cover to their own cars or down the street, and the outsiders had been caught in the mad rush of the customers. Not one of the outsiders had volunteered that he or she had seen anyone who could have been one of the killers.

Mora went back to the statements of the customers. The immediate reaction for many had been sheer, overwhelming fright. They had all been drinking. They knew the reputation of the bar; many had been there on other nights when other men had been killed. Bullets and knives had flashed in La Tortuga on several occasions. No one wanted to be caught in a cross fire of rival drug dealers or end up as the innocent victim of gang battle.

A bar customer had told the police: *"Those crazy dealers don't give a damn about anybody when they start lighting up a joint. They think it's cool, macho, and screw everybody else. We could all of been shot if the poor bastard they blew away had had time to draw his own piece."*

The sharp, earsplitting first shot also was the first indication that anything was wrong. Up until then it had been a regular night at La Tortuga—noisy, rowdy, and crowded. Several more shots immediately followed the first. A woman screamed. Then the bit of drama that crystallized the worst nightmares of many of the customers: the lights in the bar went out. The police concluded that one of the killers, maybe the one who didn't use his gun on Vigil, had wrenched open the ancient circuit box on the wall next to the booth where Vigil had been shot and thrown a switch. In the darkness, more screams, people bumping into one another, vying for the door. They rushed through the door in a chaotic stream, the killers probably among them, dragging Lorraine Garza, but in the darkness and with the collective state of panic, no one saw them.

It had been a bold, cold-blooded execution. The killers had to have been professionals, experienced, ready to kill as many people as necessary in order to get at Kiko Vigil.

Vigil's body remained. A bloody piece of paper stuck to him like a cemetery flag. In Spanish it had warned: He who wants everything will lose everything.

Mora went back to two pages that had a great deal of yellow on them. Something nagged at him that he knew he had to pay attention to before he lost it completely. Buried deep in an interviewing officer's notes, a witness offhandedly commented that when he rushed from the bar and burst through the door, he saw a wheelchair. He thought that was strange, but what about that night wasn't strange? The witness had dashed to the end of the block and down the next street without looking back. He returned later, after several police cars had screeched to the scene, and eventually gave a statement.

Mora's insides rumbled. Again he read the statement. His face wrinkled. He set the report aside, rifled through several pages in the first pile of statements he had previously reviewed. Something about one of them . . .

He lifted a report from the table. Officer Eugene Nieto had talked to several of the outsiders. In Mora's opinion, he hadn't done a very good job. The interviews were sketchy and incomplete, often including the cop's own observations and conclusions rather than those of the interviewees. The rambling narratives had few meaningful details. Still, there was something.

According to Officer Nieto, two males, one apparently Hispanic and the other apparently Anglo, had arrived after the shooting. The Hispanic, who identified himself as

"Frankie Johns," stated before he had been asked any question that he and his friend had been on the street and hadn't seen anything that happened in the bar. Nieto had scribbled three sentences at the end of his report.

This officer recognized the two as street persons who panhandle and hustle tourists for change, without long-term residences or stable employment. They had been drinking, and this officer concluded that they were unreliable as witnesses. They were not coherent, and additionally they stated they had not seen anything in the bar.

Mora saw no addresses or phone numbers for the two "street persons" anywhere on the report. That was the total of the statement that Nieto had taken from the two men. At the top of the page, Nieto had noted that the Hispanic was in a wheelchair.

Danny Mora returned to the first report, the initial reference to a wheelchair. He looked over his list of names. The statement had been taken from Rafael Soto, a bail bondsman. Soto's business phone number had been included in the statement. It was late, but Mora assumed the bondsman kept late hours, just like private investigators. He dialed the number.

On the third ring, a male voice said, "EZ Bail Bonds. What is it?"

Mora responded, "Hello, Mr. Soto?"

"Yeah, this is Soto. What do you want?"

The voice sounded impatient and rushed.

Mora thought he would have better luck if he gave the bondsman a story that offered the choice of answering quickly now or spending more time later in a lengthy interview.

"This is Detective Martínez at Homicide with the Denver police."

"Crap! What is it now? Who's run? It was that damn Dewey Gibson, wasn't it? I knew it! That sonofabitch!"

"No, no. This isn't about one of your clients."

"Then what is it? I'm kind of busy here."

Mora assumed he wouldn't get far playing tough cop with the experienced bondsman.

"I understand, Mr. Soto. Too much damn paperwork anymore. As it is, I don't want to take up too much of your time. I'm working on the Francisco Vigil murder, from about six months ago, in the Tortuga Bar?"

Heavy breathing over the phone line told Mora that Soto was tired or stressed, maybe both. Soto said, "Yeah, what about it? I thought you guys were done with that. I already told you everything I seen. Christ, man, it's been so long, I don't even remember what I did tell you the first time."

"Yes, yes. I know. It has been a while. I've read your report. I got just a few questions that I need to ask to nail down my part in this case. I can come over there and we can spend some time going over these, or—"

"Oh, man, what did you say your name was? Martínez, right? Look, *primo,* I ain't got that much time. I should be home in bed. I got to be in court in the morning for one of my clients and then I got people coming in to see me about a brother who got busted tonight, you know, that kind of stuff. It's my business. Maybe we can do this some other day?"

Mora hesitated before he answered. The heavy breathing increased in tempo. Mora said, "I don't think I can wait. This is kind of important."

"Well, how about right here on the phone? What you need to know?"

Mora counted. One thousand one. One thousand two.

He said, "It's not very official over the phone."

"Hey, we'll talk now, and if you still need something, then we can set an appointment." The volume in Soto's voice had inched higher. "How about that? I doubt I can add anything to what I already said. I answered questions for hours to another cop right after the shooting. Damn, this is the last time I try to help you guys!"

The name stared at Mora from the report.

"Detective Harris?"

"What? Oh, yeah, Harris," answered Soto, hopeful that there might be a way out of a time-consuming interview. "Why don't you talk to him? I told Harris everything."

"Yeah, like I said, I've seen your report."

Mora paused again as though he was thinking over some way to give Soto a break.

The long night and the intrusive phone call finally got to Soto. He shouted, "I got customers waiting here, buddy! Can we get this over with or what?"

Mora heaved a big sigh, as though being a police detective had to be the most frustrating job a man could have.

"Okay, okay. Easy, bud. Let's see how far we can get. I'm interested in the wheelchair that you mentioned to Detective Harris. Was there somebody with the chair?"

"Guy in the wheelchair? Sure. Screwed up my leg. Creep was right in the way when I came tearing ass through the door. On the street. Ran right into him, jacked up my ankle. Looked like his chair got knocked over. I was try-ing to get out of the way of the bullets, you know? So I guess I shouldn't say it, but I didn't stop to see what happened to him or to help him up. I kept expecting a bullet to get me in the back, you know? I split around the block. Later, when I come back, I seen the guy talking to a cop, so I figured he was all right."

"You knocked him out of the chair?"

Soto shouted again. "No way, man! He was already out of the chair when I bumped him. He was like on the street, squirming around. What is this? What's this got to do with anything? What the hell, man?"

"Well, you know what? You already helped out a lot, and now I got another call. Thanks for your help, Mr. Soto."

Mora hung up.

He wrote down Nieto's full name and the number he had scribbled on his report. Tomorrow, in the sunlight, without any subterfuge, the private investigator would talk to Officer Nieto. The cop had recognized the man in the wheelchair, at least from seeing him on the street. Maybe he knew where Mora could find him. Danny Mora wanted to ask the man in the wheelchair a couple of questions. The investigator wondered what the man had done if he had, in fact, been knocked to the ground by the frightened bar customers. Did he get back in his chair and roll away from the bar afraid, confused, and useless as a witness, like all the others? Or did he have to lie on the ground and wait for someone to help him? How long did he lie in the street, and what had he seen from his vantage point on the grimy asphalt?

Daniel Mora's eyes wandered over the papers and files that he had collected on the Vigil case. The glare and flicker of his fluorescent lighting agitated him, and he stood, walked across the room, and hit the switch. Surrounded by shadows and a gray slash of moonlight that slipped through a gap in the blinds, Daniel Mora fingered the crime scene photographs that Robert Spann had secured for him. He moved to the sliver of light near the window. In one of the photographs, Vigil's bloody, tormented corpse stretched across the litter-strewn floor of La Tortuga, his face wrenched in agony. He walked back to the table and pulled from the box another photograph. The woman's openmouthed smile stood out in the picture. Her lips formed a kiss for the camera. She wore a two-piece swimsuit that covered very little, and she sat on a beach chair, undeniably enjoying herself. No one else was in the picture, although an ocean rolled away from her in the background. Mora turned the picture over and again read the words that had been scribbled on the back of the photo.

Victor. Un recuerdo del día que celebramos su gran victoria para Elías. Con cariño, Lorraine. He translated as he read: A memory of the day we celebrated your great victory for Elías. With affection, Lorraine.

Ah, Victor and his penchant for pictures of beautiful women in suggestive poses. You'd think he would have learned his lesson. The memento from Mrs. Garza could have been trouble for Delgado if anyone had ever wondered about the complex nature and true extent of his relationship with his Mexican clients. But then, Victor Delgado had a bad habit of crossing the thin line between clients and conflicts of interest.

The private investigator placed the photographs on the table. His question for Officer Nieto had become the most important question that Mora had to ask six months after the murder of Kiko Vigil: Where could he find the "street person" Frankie Johns?

11

Four men in the booth in the corner spoke loudly and energetically about their jobs, their families, and the arrogant and rude ways of the Americans. Very few of the other customers in the diner understood Spanish, and so very few of the customers understood any of the talk of the four men. Some resented the foreign language, regarded it as an intrusion in the routine of their breakfasts, an insult to the illusion they held about their country and its people. They frowned and shook their heads and tried to ignore the babble.

Tomás Chávez saw the reactions and he, too, shook his head. He had written about the phenomenon he was witnessing. He once had championed what he called the coming cacophony of tongues, the premonitory symbol of the browning of the United States that many residents of the country were not prepared for and ill equipped to deal with in any reasonable fashion. To see it in action was both a vindication and a stab in the heart. He wanted to shout to those who clucked their teeth and skewed their eyes: *"Get with the program! The tidal wave is gathering force, and you had better learn to swim with it or be prepared to take a last deep gulp of air and hold your breath for as long as you can tread water."*

Patricia Montelibre interrupted his silent diatribe.

"Did you hear what I said? What are you thinking about?"

He forced a smile. "Excuse me. I got lost in a train of thought that I've been working on for a piece. Sorry, it was rude of me."

"You blocked out everything. Does that happen often?"

"More than I care to admit. I couldn't work my way through a polite conversation with another person if my soul depended on it."

"Well, I'm not worried about your soul, Tomás. Now, the rest of you . . ."

Things were happening too fast. Although he hadn't made any final decision and the Catholic guilt daily built up within him like sediment on the bottom of a scummy lake, he had arranged to talk with a lawyer about a divorce, someone Moony had recommended. He forced himself to deal with Lydia about possessions that he hadn't realized he'd left behind until he couldn't find them. The terms for the apartment weren't final, but he moved in with the manager's assurance that a lease was forthcoming. He wasn't sure he was doing this right. Someone should write a manual for middle-aged guys who finally jumped ship. He needed advice on lawyers, new digs, old friends, negotiating with his soon-to-be ex, what to say at work, etc., etc., etc. Someone should write that book.

A man dressed in muddy work clothes passed by their booth and stopped.

"Patty, how are you? How is your mother? I haven't seen her for years. Please tell her hello."

Patricia returned the hello, and the man walked off without an introduction to Tomás.

"You seem to have many friends."

Her smile twisted into a shrug. She said, "I was born in Denver, been here all my life except when I went away to school. Some of the crowd I hung around with when I was a kid are still hanging around, and we see each other at events, parties, that kind of thing. And then, there are the people I know through Carlos."

"Carlos?" Tomás realized as soon as he heard himself repeat the man's name that his voice had a tone that wasn't right. There was no good reason for it. Much slower, he added, "Who's that?"

"My older brother." Her entire body straightened. Tomás heard pride in her voice.

"I guess I don't know much about your family."

Her head bobbed up and down.

"They haven't come up in our conversation. I should tell you about Carlos?"

He carefully watched her as she spoke, and for what seemed like the hundredth time that morning, he was excited by her, buoyed by the strength he saw in her. The distance between him and Lydia had manifested itself in the lack of communication at the dining-room table and the lack of contact in the bedroom. He was ready for communication and more. From the shoulder-length hair that fell smooth and straight across Patricia's neck, to her large, brown eyes that didn't flinch when he stared at her, that, in fact, stared back with an intensity that he swore he had never found in anyone else—Tomás Chávez was smitten.

"My older brother was political, what we used to call an activist. He died in a, uh, an incident. An explosion in a house he was living in. He and several others who were always accused of making trouble lived together in a house on the West Side that was kind of like a commune—a leftist Chicano commune where the residents studied the writings of Chairman Mao and read biographies of Che Guevara. One night the place went up in flames after something exploded, and my brother, Carlos, and two others were killed. The police said they had been making bombs and blew themselves up. They could never prove that, and I and almost every other Chicano in the city didn't believe it. Carlos wasn't a bomber, but he's been labeled a terrorist ever since his death. Before that, really. Like I said, he was always being accused of something by the cops. Nothing they could ever prove. But anyway, from those days, a lot of my brother's old friends remember me as his little sister and they still treat me that way. That guy who was just in here was one of Carlos's buddies. They watch out for me and keep their eye on me, for Carlos's sake, I guess. You know how it is around here. Denver is a big city, but it's like a small town in a lot of ways, including the circle of old friends who seem to always turn up when you least expect them."

"Carlos Montelibre!" He stopped himself from whistling. "Sure. I remember that explosion. I didn't know Carlos was your brother."

"Does that mean you'd rather not finish breakfast with me? Afraid the FBI may have a tail on me?"

He laughed, reached across the counter, and grabbed her hand.

"I guess it's too late for that. By now everyone in the state must know that you and I have been spending time together."

She smiled.

"Oh, yeah, everyone. Including your wife?"

Tomás tried to change the subject.

"Look, I've about had it with this coffee. Let's get out of here, okay? Didn't you say you had something to do?"

She frowned, and he immediately regretted his words.

Patricia said, "Talk about the brush-off. But really, Tomás. It's summer. I'm taking one class for my master's. It's not like I have a full schedule. But if you insist, we can leave."

She gathered her keys and the newspaper that had sat undisturbed between them while they talked.

"I didn't mean it that way, Patricia." He thought quickly, tried to recover the moment. "If you don't have anything to do, maybe you can help me unpack and figure out what I'll need for my place. I'm not very good at this sort of thing."

"If you want some help, sure. Come on. I'll follow you."

His heart beat in his ears and his breathing escalated. His clumsy mistake hadn't sent her away. He took one last drink from his coffee, then told himself to relax. This just might work out.

■

They rubbed and groped each other amid boxes and scattered clothes in the front room of the apartment before they found their way to the bed. She laughed and giggled while

Tomás struggled out of his coat, tie, and pants. He couldn't keep his hands off her skin, cool against his. His fingers traveled the bright tan line around the sulky darkness of her hips, while his mouth found her neck, shoulders, and breasts. Tomás lost himself in a montage of lips, nipples, legs. She cooed in his ear, telling him how good he felt, how much she had wanted him since the night of the party. She moved away and he was confused for an instant, questioning her intentions, imagining the cruelest of jokes that she could inflict on him. Then her lips brushed against him. He reached down and slowly moved his hands through her hair. He watched her and she looked up at him, their eyes locked on each other. The guttural sounds of uninhibited sex replaced her childlike giggles. He twisted in the bed and moved down her belly. She trembled and moaned and lost her hold on him, but he didn't care. He abandoned himself to her, drinking her, freezing her image in his heart.

Neither one heard the telephone ring, nor the message that was left for Tomás on his newly installed answering machine. They didn't ignore Daniel Mora, they simply never heard him until much later, when Tomás finally emerged from the bedroom and saw the blinking light on his machine. By that time, Tomás Chávez was in love.

■

Patricia surprised herself, although she couldn't deny that her infatuation for Tomás had quickly transformed into a yearning and then a lingering fever. She had never thrown herself at anyone like she knew she was doing with Tomás. The fling with Victor Delgado had been the culmination of a long, well thought out campaign engineered by Victor and obvious to Patricia. When she gave in to him, it was more a reward for his perseverance than the result of an overwhelming emotion to couple with him.

Her feelings for Tomás were different, completely different. Silvia had been right, of course, at first. She *had* flirted with him. She had been attracted by his reputation and the universal taboo he represented—married man. But after only a few hours with him, watching him work his mind, observing how he took the time to see where she was coming from, her attraction had moved well beyond the infatuation stage. She had no explanation, she wouldn't try to craft one for the benefit of Silvia or her other friends. She had surprised herself when she accepted his invitation to go with him to his apartment, but Silvia wouldn't believe that. Her surprise increased when she moved toward him for that first kiss, but all the surprises stopped when she accepted that she was excited by him, that she wanted him, and that her desire might be regrettable later but right then, right at the moment when she grabbed his hand and led him to the bedroom, right then, her mind was clear and she was amazingly calm. They moved together so naturally, and he made her feel so good that she floated away into the zone that she had known only a few times in her sexual life. She didn't think of anyone or anything else other than what she could do to make him feel as wonderful as he was making her feel. He was a patient man, knowing and sincere in his movements. His caresses invited a response, and her body willingly complied. For her it was natural and logical to move up and down his body, to love him as intimately as she could, as privately as she could make the act, as though it was a secret within herself that she deliberately and succinctly revealed to him, bit by bit. She watched him as his excitement grew, and that made her that much more excited. She felt his thighs tense, rubbed his rigid back muscles. She gave up completely and flew with him as he increased his urgency, devouring her as though he were a drowning man and she was his river.

A completely random, irrelevant thought floated from somewhere through her lust-smogged consciousness. A damn ex-priest! She arched her back and smiled. Oh, you damn ex-priest.

12

Charles Compeán slumped on the overstuffed couch. He clutched a bottle of Presidente brandy. He raised his head only to push a drink through clenched teeth. The liquor burned his split lip. One eye was swollen shut. Scrapes, bruises, and welts marked his face with a crazy quilt of pain.

Silvia Compeán had been crying for more than an hour, but he would never know that. There were no flowing tears or strident hysterics. She cried without making a sound, without revealing that she was broken down. She hid the agonized edge of the despair that cut her heart in two.

She forced her words.

"It can never be over for you. How can you go on doing this? Don't you know what you are doing to me? To yourself? I can't continue this way."

He sobbed. His pathetic voice croaked through his throbbing, bleeding mouth.

"I know, Silvia. I know, don't you think I damn well know all that! What the hell can I do? I've tried everything, everything. What the hell can I do?"

She had no pity for him. That had ended years before when she had first learned what kind of man Charles Compeán really was beneath the happy-go-lucky exterior and success-laden trappings.

"It's the lie you insist on living, Charles. And the perverse way you have to exorcise what you think is your own private demon. When you had to use Delgado to get you out of your last trouble, wasn't that enough? Wasn't it enough what I had to do to keep Delgado's mouth shut? Wasn't that enough!"

He recoiled in humiliation from her voice. He cowered on the couch. The arrest in the dingy rest room in the bar near Capitol Hill—that should have been enough. The massive cover-up that he had to engineer, that only a man with his wealth could finance so that newspapers and TV stations didn't trumpet the news about his arrest. The desperate employment of Victor Delgado, a man who had no qualms about manipulating the case so that it would never see the light of day—that should have been enough. And when Delgado balked, when he threatened to bury Charles's carefully groomed image unless he received special payment—that should have been more than enough to teach Charles the most difficult lesson in his life. But he had paid Delgado. He gave him what he wanted. He gave him Silvia, and she had done it for him, she had paid the attorney his monstrous fee. He had burned Delgado's disgusting photographs of the manner of payment that had been extracted from his wife, but he could never burn away the shame.

Silvia stood over her cringing husband.

"Charles, pull yourself together. We have to take care of things. We have to start fixing this mess. I guess you can't help yourself. This . . . this boy, young man, whoever he is. Pay him what he wants. We have no choice. But he has to leave town. You have to make sure that he's gone. Make the arrangements, get somebody to take him away, to dump him anywhere else—in hell for all I care."

He stared at her. She was right. He had no choice. And he would never do it again. He would never proposition someone that way again, in one of those disgusting places. He would be true and faithful to Silvia. He loved her; he knew that, she knew that. This other was just a weakness, an addiction that he had to give up, that he knew he would give up. For Silvia.

She said, "From now on, Charles, you and I are finished." His jaw twitched. His nervous tic was another sign that he was about to fall apart completely.

She quickly said, "No, Charles, I'm not leaving. All the shit you put me through, and I still won't leave. I'm condemned to stay here. You've known that for years. But not as your wife. We may live in the same house, we may pretend in front of the others, but you and I are over. I've never understood your needs, and I refuse to try anymore. When you need that kind of sex, you will take care of it here, in this house, when I am gone. You will stop acting like an animal, prowling the darkest parts of the city for your thrills. You will make arrangements just like you do with any other business situation, and you will quit the charade. This could have been dealt with years ago if only you had been strong enough to admit the truth, but strength was never one of your virtues, was it, Charles? You're a weak man, and I must be a weak woman to put up with all the pain you've caused me. But you and I are through. Make no mistake about that. And if you get involved in one more smutty mistake, I will leave and to hell with you."

She walked out of the room, and Charles Compeán sat in darkness, staring at a vague spot on the carpet that he had never noticed before. He tried to concentrate on that spot because it was the only thing that made sense to him right then.

■

The tired voice wasn't immediately recognizable. The words came across the line in a lethargic, almost inaudible jumble.

"I have to trust someone. It's . . . very delicate. I hope I can trust you? Only the strictest confidentiality?"

There it was again, that same question mark about preserving client confidences that Robert Spann had insinuated when he had hired Mora.

The detective said what he had to. "My business lives or dies based on what my clients say about my services. Everything I do for you, everything I learn, everything you tell me, is a matter of trust that I will not break, as long as it's not illegal. What is it that I can do for you, Mr. Compeán?"

"I remembered your name because of your past association with Victor Delgado."

Mora rolled his eyes.

"If this has anything to do with Victor Delgado, then you'll have to find yourself someone else."

"No, no. Wait. What I mean is, you worked for him when he represented me on a matter that I'd rather not get into now. That's where I learned about you and your work. You were his investigator. And that was when he uh . . . uh. I . . . ah, I . . . how much of this do you want to hear?"

Danny Mora decided to help out the wealthy entrepreneur. He filled in the details for the reluctant Charles Compeán.

"Delgado was your attorney in a case involving you and a young, very young, man. It took a great deal of persuasion—money and certain promises to a handful of politicians—to keep your name out of the papers and off the court dockets. Just when all the details had been lined up, your lawyer decided to squeeze you for something else. He threatened to pull out of the case and blow the lid on the cover-up unless you substantially enhanced his fee."

"Yes, that's it."

"And he wanted sex with your wife."

Compeán groaned over the phone. Mora continued his litany of facts as though he were dictating a memo to a file.

"Apparently you agreed to all the terms because I've never seen you on the ten o'clock news except when you attend charity balls with your gracious wife."

"Maybe this was a mistake." Mora could feel Compeán's desperation over the phone line. "I thought I could trust you because you had a falling-out with Delgado, and since you never said anything to anybody, and you never . . ."

"No, Mr. Compeán, I never put the bite on you to keep my mouth shut. And yes, Delgado and I did have a falling-out, as you call it. I didn't know what he was up to with you. I never did anything on your case except run down background information on the police officers who arrested you. But afterward, when it was all over, I did see the photos of your wife, Mr. Compeán. When I saw those, and Delgado bragged to me about what he had done, I quit him. I won't have anything to do with him now. And he won't deal with me. He doesn't trust me, you see. I know too much about the way he does business."

But, Mora admitted to himself, his knowledge of the way Delgado did business had paid off in Delgado's cooperation with the Garza file. Victor was such an ass, a coward, basically. Tapes, photos, who knew what else. The man loved images of himself. All that preserved information could be dangerous. Apparently the lawyer didn't fear the consequences.

Delgado should have been stripped of his license to practice law years ago. The women who had been coerced by Delgado, usually emotionally scarred divorce clients or the intimidated girlfriends of criminal defendant clients, should have complained to the state supreme court and had him forced out of lawyering. That hadn't happened.

Compeán said gratefully, "Yes, yes. That's what I had hoped for, I guess. I need to hire you, Mr. Mora. I need to make sure that a person leaves town and won't be coming back. I want you to watch him and to make sure that he ends up where I'm sending him. I don't want him coming back."

"Is this person blackmailing you, Mr. Compeán?"

"No! I mean, yes, he is, but that's not it. I'm getting rid of him, and I need someone to make sure he follows through with his part, that's all."

"You should inform the police. They will deal with him. You can't be sure that no matter what you do now, this person won't come back one day and ask for more. If you go to the police—"

"I can't go to the police! Don't you understand that? I can't be involved! It's not an option, not right now. I just want him out of town."

Mora heard the man's labored breathing, the desperation in his voice. Mora had no respect for Compeán. He had betrayed, then bartered away his wife. And now he wanted help.

Compeán whispered, "Can you do that? Can you get this man out of town?"

Compeán had lied for his entire life—to everyone in his life who mattered, from his parents and brothers and sisters to his wife to himself. He had built a world of fear and self-loathing. That made him susceptible to parasites such as the man Compeán wanted Mora to escort out of town and deliver a strong message to about never showing his face in Denver again. Compeán had influence and close, trusted ties to power and money. Yet his inability to accept himself for what he was had made him weak and vulnerable.

"I'll do the job, Mr. Compeán. With a few conditions. I'll scare the guy off, but I will only go so far. I won't be involved in any payoff to cops or district attorneys or politicians. I won't falsify evidence or manufacture a story for you. And I won't be a party to anything that involves the kind of thing that happened before, to your wife. Do you understand?"

Maybe Compeán would surprise Mora, maybe he had

dug up the missing part of his soul that he seemed so ready to forget about, that part that had to do with integrity. Maybe Charles Compeán would tell Danny Mora to forget it.

"Yes, Mora. I understand. I'll come by your office tomorrow with the details and your retainer."

The phone clicked.

13

Danny Mora's neighbors struggled valiantly to keep their lawns alive for the remaining months of the summer. The trappings of the season, from the weekly yard sale at the corner house to the discarded wrappers from La Paletería Mexicana, had come to include numerous patches of yellow, thirsty grass. Sprinklers and hoses were moved and rearranged at a steady clip up and down the block. His neighbor to the south, Mrs. Herrera, maintained a stream running across her sidewalk, and a puddle of muddy water had collected where her driveway merged into the street.

Danny Mora had watched these hot-weather routines for years. He did his share of trying to keep the neighborhood neat, trimmed, and green. Invariably, his lawn was the driest and the thinnest. How could he compete with the widows who spent their days working the earth of their yards or the group of Mexican laborers who shared a house and watered each section of their luxurious lawn with detailed, measured care? He had no chance.

"You should be ashamed, Moony. Mrs. Herrera's yard looks like it could be part of the Botanic Gardens. She's going to get a court order against you—force you to either shape up your lawn or put up a ten-foot fence so no one else has to see it."

Tomás Chávez laughed at his own joke. Danny Mora couldn't help but notice that he seemed to laugh a lot more lately.

"It's not that bad. I do what I can. I'm a busy man."

Tomás flicked away Danny's rationalization with a quick head shake. "I'm glad you could fit us in tonight. Patricia's eager to meet you. And I think you'll like her."

Mora had agreed with less enthusiasm than Tomás wanted. He expected that the dinner would be uncomfortable for him. He had known Lydia Chávez for years, and he considered her a friend. The separation, and Tomás's new fling—everything had changed, everything had suddenly become more complicated.

"You've never met Patricia, right?"

"No. I've heard of her, know a few things about her—teacher, active in city politics. I've seen her with Delgado, and that didn't make a good first impression. But I'm giving her a chance."

Tomás grimaced at the mention of the lawyer, but he knew that Mora hadn't intended anything by his remark. Moony recited facts about people that way; it was a habit from his profession. There had never been much subtlety in Moony's character, only the dark, hard edge that set him apart from everyone else. Tomás had seen it since they were children, and he had no explanation for his friend.

The tiny, almost imperceptible flare in Tomás's eyes signaled Danny that he had to say something to make the night easier.

"She must be special. She comes from a big, solid family. Carlos was a good guy."

Tomás smiled. The telephone rang.

Danny answered and immediately was serious.

"Hello, Lydia. Yes, I know. It has been a while."

Chávez watched as Danny Mora maneuvered his conversation with Lydia so that he wouldn't hurt her feelings or embarrass his friend. It was a painful exercise for Mora. Chávez caught his attention with a wave of his hand, pointed at his watch, and held up seven fingers to indicate that he would see him later at dinner. Danny Mora frowned, then turned his attention back to Lydia Chávez.

■

The night had caught up with Victor Delgado before he was ready for it. He switched on his desk lamp but didn't bother to turn on the overhead office light. Whatever he had to see was all in front of him, if only he could recognize it.

He muttered to himself.

Friday night, and I'm stuck in my office. That damn Gonzales! Waits until the last day to let me know that his client won't go along with the deal. Deposition for Monday, and I can't find my client! Why do I put up with this crap!

Sometimes it all seemed like a silly, nonsensical game.

Doctors' reports and hospital records lay scattered across his desk. He needed to be intimately familiar with the medical file of his client because there was a question about the seriousness of the injury that everyone admitted took place. The case should have been wrapped up weeks ago, but the insurer's lawyer—Michael Gonzales, a classmate, if you could believe that—had dicked around and put off Victor so smoothly and expertly that as the deposition approached, he felt unprepared and knew he was at a distinct disadvantage. This was his deposition, a fishing expedition against the insurance company's expert, yet it would take Victor Delgado all weekend to plow through the mound of reports, memos, x rays, and doctor's notes just so he could ask a few intelligent questions. He hated Michael Gonzales.

Through the smoke of his cigarette, Delgado stared at a report written by a doctor—he didn't understand a word of it. The paper shimmied in and out of focus; the words moved, jumped around the page. He loosened his suspenders and let them hang at the sides of his executive La-Z-Boy. It was hopeless. He couldn't do this. He would have to find a way to postpone the deposition without revealing his unpreparedness. Don't let them hear you squeal—that was supposed to be the guiding principle when you found your butt stuck in a vise.

He twisted his cigarette stub in an ashtray, rubbed his eyes with both hands, and stood. Walking around might help. Carla had been upset. He couldn't blame her. This was the third time this week that he had canceled on her. His weak promise to see her later hadn't been enough. She was history, and that made him a bit sad. The things that little lady liked to do—often in parking lots. They had made love, if you wanted to call what they did love, in the front seat of his car and against the back wall of a dark bar, surrounded by a dozen drunks who had no idea what Victor and Carla were up to. But all that was over now. That damn Gonzales!

The shadow moved against the wall and across Victor's face. He couldn't help but see it. He jerked instinctively and ducked, as though he expected something hurled at his head. He started to say something but caught himself. He dropped to his knees and crawled away from the aura of light around the desk. He heard it very clearly now. Footsteps, but he couldn't determine if the trespasser was in his office or out in the waiting area, or maybe in the hall.

He should get to the phone. How did the guy get in? What did he want? Delgado tried to think. He'd never had to deal with anything like this. An intruder in his office! He must believe no one was there. *Maybe a noise will frighten him off. If he realizes he's not alone, that might do it—probably a strung-out punk looking for quick cash or a computer that he can sell on the street for a few bucks.* Delgado calmed down a bit. He had the upper hand. The element of surprise. Now he had to use it. Crime in the city—who'd have thought that Victor Delgado, defense attorney, would be a victim? A crazy thought came to him. What if the guy was one of his own clients! Could be! Made plenty of sense. Damn, damn!

The man appeared in the doorway. He saw Delgado almost immediately, at about the same time that Delgado focused on his face. Delgado's heavy breathing, the only sound in the office, was interrupted by a sudden, intrusive pop when the man pulled the trigger on his weapon. The man released the air he had been holding in his lungs as Delgado slammed against the wall. The killer knew that

Delgado had seen him, recognized him, and that made him smile. He walked over to the squirming Delgado as the wounded man groaned in protest of what was about to happen. He stood over Victor Delgado and slowly aimed his gun. He stood at an angle to avoid the splashback. His hand holding the gun jerked. The blood spatters and the way the back of Delgado's skull exploded reminded the killer of the death of Kiko Vigil, and that seemed very appropriate.

There wouldn't be a note for this one. No one else had to learn a lesson. The killing wasn't a warning or a threat to anyone else. It had been for Victor Delgado and only Victor Delgado, and now it was done and there was no need for any theatrical notes or gory throat slashing.

He returned his gun to the holster under his jacket, looked around one more time for something to be careful about, and then walked out of the office. He grasped a miniature flashlight between his teeth as he searched the filing cabinets for the material that he wanted. Several minutes passed, filled only with the sounds of frantic paper shuffling. Spanish epithets burst from him, and the sound of his voice surprised him. He had made a mistake. He had assumed that he would find what he wanted without needing Delgado. He should have secured the papers and tapes first and then killed Delgado. His job was unfinished, and he had no one to tell him about the files or recordings.

He returned to Delgado's office, where a large circle of blood had soaked the carpet. He carefully avoided the body and the blood. He scrutinized the papers on the desk without touching them. He looked in vain for an appointment book. He scoured the office, the walls, the bookshelves, the pictures. Nothing. The beginning of something like panic crept over him. He might have to search the body, but that would court more disaster. He mentally made a note of the items on the desk: pen, overflowing ashtray, file folder, pages of reports, telephone. He looked at the walls of the office once more.

A large calendar with white squares of space for each day hung behind the desk. Most of the squares were filled with handwritten notes, scribbles and doodles. The man breathed easier. It had been there all the time, but he hadn't seen it. That's what happened when you let this shit get under your skin. He stood directly in front of the calendar and went through it, day by day, week by week, using his mouth-held light to examine Delgado's notes in each block of space.

Behind him, Delgado's body gurgled with leaking blood. The sound was faint, almost nothing, but he heard it. He resented the sound.

Four days ago, Monday, July 27. Victor Delgado had a lot of questions on that particular day.

Call Gonzales?!

Carla?

Mora: Garza?

Reschedule Perkins?

The man flicked off the flashlight and let out a sigh. His work had only begun.

■

Patricia Montelibre watched with keen interest the inter-action between Tomás Chávez and his friend Danny Mora. She liked to observe men with men because it revealed so much about what she thought was the problem between men and women. Men played mental and linguistic games with each other that fulfilled functions that with women were taken care of by means of regular conversation. The degree of complexity of these games varied depending on the closeness of the particular men, but they were always present, usually unacknowledged by the men. She quickly concluded that Tomás and Danny had a repertoire of insider messages and jokes that were triggered with signals that they had used over the years and that were hidden to all others. The code must have started when they were children together, and now neither one thought anything about it. It was as natural as the easy laughter the men had with each other, and Patricia inwardly shrugged at her bit of jealousy about their friendship.

Their mutual respect tinged everything they did in each other's company, from their greetings to the topics of conversation to the way they treated third parties who happened to be in the same room with them.

Tomás was intense and intellectual, while Danny was intense and physical. Tomás listened closely to every word spoken to him, and he answered with deliberation and well-chosen words. She had learned in the short time they had been together that his personality ran deep and quiet, a challenge to tap into, certainly, but an attainable goal for the right woman. Danny's intensity, however, was a dark, barely contained force, an intimidating, wary nature that made Patricia think no one really knew Danny Mora very well.

Tomás had arranged a buffet table piled with the fixings needed for fajitas and tacos. He had cooked marinated chicken on a gas grill on the apartment patio and announced that everything was ready when the pan of rice on his stove was finally finished. The three had eagerly devoured the spicy food and quickly finished off a bottle of Chilean merlot. Tomás had opened another with the announcement that he wanted to toast "the two best friends in the world." Patricia felt her cheeks warm and she knew she had blushed. She was surprised that she was included in the same intimate, very close grouping that she was sure for years had consisted only of Danny Mora.

She let herself get caught up in the emotion of the evening. The residue of the passion she had been sharing with Tomás for the past several days and nights crept into her speech, and she giddily proclaimed to Tomás and Danny, "To Chacho and Moony, to all our friends, yours and mine, everywhere, may they be as happy as we are now!" The men shouted agreement with her sentiment, and she laughed. She had never thought of herself as such an exuberant person.

Danny reached for the bottle and filled her glass again. He would give her a chance, even though he was conflicted about Tomás and his romantic fling. He liked her honesty and her quick mind. She was, of course, the type of woman that Tomás would find attractive, although Mora remained ambivalent about her in that way. Since she had celebrated friendship with her toast, he asked about her friends.

"Who are your closest friends, Patricia? Besides Tomás, I mean. Perhaps I know some of them. I've been in Denver all my life. Tomás must have filled you in on all the gritty details of our sordid pasts, no doubt."

She assumed that the wine had made Mora more approachable. She answered, "I'm a native, too. A rare breed anymore. But it means that a lot of the people I know have been around my family for years—my parents and my brother."

Mora nodded.

"Yes, your brother. Carlos. I admired him for his commitment. A man with a vision. Talk about a rare breed! It was a tragic loss when he was killed."

She felt the heaviness in her throat that the memory of Carlos always created.

"I never really got over his death—I'm sure you understand." Tomás saw the pride again as she talked about her brother. "He was a special man, but to me he was just my older brother, and that's the way I miss him. He happened to be a public figure that others also miss, but that's in a different way."

Danny remembered the story. He said, "That day, when the building exploded and then the fire that burned out of control through the old warehouses. Many of us in Denver at that time will never forget the details. For some of us, it's more vivid than anything else in our youth. Carlos, the woman, Inés Carrillo, and the third man, Alfred, what was it?"

"Leal, his name was Alfred Leal." She answered quickly. "They were friends of Carlos. Inés was his girlfriend. Carlos told me they were talking about getting married. Leal, I didn't know that well. He was new to the circle that moved around Carlos. Apparently very zealous, and a long history of community activism. He and Carlos hit it off well, I do remember that. The police concluded that they had been making bombs or storing dynamite. That was not what they were doing. I was convinced then and I still am that Carlos was murdered, and the others were also victims simply because they happened to be with Carlos. But back then, no one would listen to us, the family or friends. So today, if anyone thinks about Carlos, it's always as the terrorist who killed himself. I hate that."

The conversation had gone to a darker place than Danny had intended. He looked to Tomás for help.

Tomás, sitting next to Patricia, picked up on his cue.

"She has a bevy of friends throughout this town. Good people! I was introduced to many of them at Silvia's party, where we met, Patricia and me, I mean. Turned out to be a great party, at least from my point of view."

Mora smiled.

"Yes, the infamous party. I've heard about it. From you, Tomás. I'm sorry, Silvia who? I don't think I was ever told a last name."

Patricia responded, eager to rid herself of the melancholy. "Compeán. A good friend. Since college. Silvia Compeán, and her husband, too, of course. Charles."

Warily Mora asked, "Charles Compeán, the businessman? That Compeán?"

"Yes. Why? Do you know him?"

The wine forced out the words quicker than Mora could think about them.

"Quite a crowd you hang with. Assholes with money and nothing better to do than waste it and waste themselves. Can't say I have any respect for people like that."

Patricia stared at him, dumbfounded by his remarks. She muttered rather lamely, "Are you joking?"

Before Mora could answer, Chávez shouted at him.

"Hey, man! What the hell is this? Since you're so concerned about respect, why not show some for Patricia? These are her friends, Danny!"

Although he had agreed to work for him, Danny did

not like Charles Compeán, and what he knew about Silvia made him think that he wouldn't like her, either. She had let herself be used by her husband. With a rapidness that had caused him trouble before, he had made up his mind about the Compeáns and their friends. There was nothing authentic about these people, and Mora had to admit to himself that he had let Charles drag him down into his grimy life. His resentment about Compeán had carried over to a bad taste in his mouth for himself.

"Tomás, I'm not talking about your girlfriend. I don't even know her. It's these other people, the people she has around her. You know how they are! Phonies, frauds!"

Chávez grabbed Mora by the arm. He spoke with slow, deliberate words.

"Cool it! I'm going to believe you're drunk. But you have to stop. You and your bullshit. Same old crap from you, except this time you've insulted Patricia. Apologize."

Patricia had to say something.

"Tomás, it's okay. Forget it. Let's just call it a night."

Danny Mora interrupted her.

"I'll leave you two. I've got to get ready for a trip, anyway."

Before Patricia or Tomás could do anything else, Mora had rushed out the front door, slamming it behind him.

Patricia hugged Tomás and said, "I'm sorry. I didn't mean to get between you two. I . . ."

"It's not you. Danny gets like that. The jerk never did apologize."

She thought he should wait for excuses for Mora's behavior before he regretted any conclusions he might jump to. She hoped that they could all be friends again.

And ironically, she agreed with Danny, to a certain extent. Charles Compeán could act like a fool who had too much money. Silvia was his saving grace.

She said, "Does he steam up like that often?"

Tomás shook his head.

"Not anymore. He's calmed down, I guess is the way to put it. He's quick to judge, and he's not very tolerant. He doesn't trust people with a lot of money. It's an old bias from when we were kids and neither one of us had anything. I guess some of the things he's been through have jaded him so much that he doesn't know how to cope sometimes. I'm sorry for you, sorry you had to get dragged through it."

"You're still friends, aren't you? This won't end that, will it?"

He tried to smile. "Of course not! We go through this every once in a while. Danny Mora has a bad disposition, an ugly temper, and ugly manners, but I love him like a brother. It will be all right, don't worry."

The catch in his voice told her otherwise.

14

By the time Flight 704 landed at the San Antonio airport, Danny Mora could almost stomach Gary Jenson's smell. It was the smell of a terrible hangover, the residue from a long night of jaw-twisting meth, anonymous sex, and sporadic blood. It was an acrid, metallic smell, and the first hour in the plane had been foul and torturous for Danny. Jenson's going-away party lingered in the air over his head and shoulders and in the folds of the greasy, stained denim jacket that lay in a bundle at Jenson's feet. When, at last, Mora had desensitized to the odor, his mind still reeled at Jenson himself: the physical wreck of humanity who sold himself on street corners, who fed his body various poisons, who treated friends and enemies in the same smarmy, contemptuous manner—all in the interest of the elusive good time, the high that was supposed to be so much better than the last one.

The only tickets available for Mora's rushed schedule and one-day turnaround had required a stopover in Houston. The men hadn't said a word to each other on the plane or in the Houston airport. They landed in San Antonio in silence.

Mora hung by Jenson's side as they exited the plane. They walked stride for stride through the long carpeted corridor, ignoring the southwestern art that hung on the walls. Compared with Denver International, the San Antonio airport looked almost deserted.

Jenson mumbled, "I can get out by myself. I don't need your baby-sitting anymore."

Mora grabbed Jenson's elbow and pinched the skinny man's arm between his fingers. Jenson yelped. Mora forced Jenson through the entrance to a rest room. A half dozen men stood at the urinals. The dim lighting worked to Mora's advantage.

Jenson hollered, "Let go of me, asshole! I don't need to piss!"

Mora twisted Jenson's arm behind his back and shoved him into one of the stalls. He gambled that the airport surveillance cameras' invasions of privacy stopped at the stall door.

As Jenson tumbled against the toilet, Mora said, "Shut up and listen."

The men at the urinals were surprised by the shouting. They quickly finished their business, zipped their pants, grabbed their luggage, and scurried out. A man in jeans and a cowboy hat stopped at the stall door, then changed his mind and walked away.

Jenson squealed like a rat strung up by its tail.

"Quit hurting me! Get your hands off me!"

Mora pushed Jenson against the toilet and bent him backward at the knees. Mora squeezed his neck, then released. Squeezed, released. Jenson's eyes flared open as his throat was alternately shut, then opened.

Mora spoke quietly, directly into Jenson's sour-smelling, splotchy face.

"I'm going to tell you one more time. So there are no misunderstandings. You've been paid. You are never to show your face in Denver again. Never. I see you, find your ass anywhere in Colorado, you'll get hurt. Don't even think about Charles Compeán. Your hustling, blackmailing days in Denver are history. Do your act somewhere else. Understand?"

Tears welled up in Jenson's eyes. Red spots dotted his forehead and cheeks. He slowly, painfully moved his head up and down.

Mora said, "Good."

He released the man's windpipe. Jenson sucked in air as quickly as he could. Mora watched the coughing, blubbering man for several minutes.

Finally Jenson said, "You got no right. You . . ."

Danny Mora threw his fist into Gary Jenson's belly. Jenson doubled over, then fell to his knees. He cried quietly, tears and mucus mingling with the thin layer of moisture on the bathroom's floor.

Mora ignored the writhing man. He spoke more to himself than to Jenson.

"It's not a question of right. It's what you have to do. Do not screw up. You do not want to screw up."

He left Jenson squirming on the floor of the cubicle.

He stopped at a sink, ran soap and water over his hands, stared in the mirror, and splashed cold water on his face.

Several men entered the rest room, glanced at Jenson's feet protruding from under the stall's door, then went on with relieving themselves.

Mora reentered the corridor and broke into a brisk trot in the direction of a yellow sign that blinked *Cantina-Cantina*. He had a two-hour wait for his return flight to Denver. He found an empty stool at the bar and quickly ordered from the woman who served the drinks. He immediately downed a shot of expensive whiskey, then almost as quickly he drank half of a glass of beer. The exorcism of Gary Jenson's smell and face and his own role in Compeán's pitiful life had begun. He scowled at his watch. Two hours might not be enough time. He drank more beer.

He never saw the two men who were quietly but efficiently ushered out of the airport by uniformed security guards. Billy Cordero and David the Dancer had worn out their reluctant welcome at the Alamo. They had tried to entertain airport visitors with sultry saxophone music and wild gyrations, but they had been forced to stop by the very serious guards. Both men asserted their constitutional rights and threatened lawsuits from the UCLA, but all they got for their protests was a free cab ride back to downtown San Antonio, paid for by Glenn Harlow, the security supervisor. Glenn didn't want any trouble in his airport. He kept a secure, usually efficient place, and it was easier for him to send the two oddballs on their way than to go through the rigmarole of arresting the men and dealing with the cops and subsequent paperwork. Twenty-five bucks for the taxi was a cheap price to pay to keep the airport quiet, safe, and respectable.

■

The man smirked inwardly at the people who expressed sadness over Delgado's death. They all knew the truth about Delgado, yet they insisted on playing this game, this mourning routine that had nothing to do with the real Delgado. But he didn't reveal any of this. These people would never know what he was thinking as he listened to the prayers and eulogies, as he offered his condolences to Delgado's so-called friends, as he stood next to the open coffin and stared at the waxy reconstructed face of the man he had killed.

You screwed up, Victor. So close to all that money, but you had to get sloppy and greedy. That was the last straw. You wanted too much. You didn't think Garza would let you play that game, did you really? What a dope! You thought you could squeeze Garza because of your childish tape recordings! I know that man; I've seen him work for years. He's got me by the balls—I don't deny it. But so what? Look where it got you, and look where it got me. Check this out, Victor. Sweat is rolling down my back—I'm wearing a black suit in this motherfucking heat. For you, Victor. That's what you're missing. It's a goddamn hot day, Victor. But not as hot as where you are, is it?

He smiled, but almost immediately caught himself. His grin changed into the thin line of concern that he had worn since he had strolled somberly through the church door. He felt sure that no one had noticed. The woman behind him coughed, and he worried that he had taken too much time at Victor's casket. He made a hurried sign of the cross and left the church.

■

Victor Delgado's funeral took place on a sweltering Thursday that began as a pleasant summer morning and ended up as an unusually muggy and uncomfortable afternoon. The Catholic church where Victor occasionally had shown up for a mass, Our Lady of Guadalupe, was packed with a sweating crowd of more than two hundred mourners—those who felt some measure of sympathy for the dead man—colleagues, opponents, judges, past girlfriends—and men and women who hated him and wanted to certify that he was, indeed, dead. The pallbearers were all members of the board of directors of the Hispanic Bar Association, an organization that Victor had paid dues to since he was in law school and for which he had once served a term as president. They all expressed that Victor Delgado was one of the "good guys," a Hispanic lawyer who never forgot his roots, who did numerous pro bono cases, was active in civic affairs, and probably would have made a good mayor, or at least a councilman. The public consensus among them, the opinion that they all voiced when asked, was that Victor's sudden, violent death was one of those off-center, unexplainable bits of evil that had nothing to do with the way the man had lived his life.

Patricia sat in the same row as Genevieve Martínez-Higgins, Clarke Higgins, and Carmen and Reymundo Fernández. Silvia and Charles Compeán were noticeably absent.

Tomás also didn't attend the services. He had begged off when Patricia asked.

"I don't know the guy, and from what I've heard

about him, I don't understand why people are so distressed by his death. But I guess it's true, only perfect people ever die."

Patricia believed it was her duty to make an appearance at the funeral. Their relationship had been only one of many for Victor, but it had been one of the lengthier ones, and she really was the closest symbol for an ex-wife that might appear dressed in black for the dead lawyer. It hadn't been that long ago that she and Victor had enjoyed each other's company, even had fun together. That was before Tomás, of course, but a hint of sadness crept into the edge of her voice, and real tears fell as a half dozen of Victor's friends and relatives responded to the priest's request for a "few words of respect." They offered their accounts of memories that were designed to induce sobbing and clearing of throats, and the crowd appropriately responded, including Patricia.

After the services, and before they climbed in their cars for the drive to the cemetery, Patricia and her friends gathered under a tree that offered shade on the edge of the church's property line. They conducted their own ceremony for Delgado. They commiserated for a man whom none of them truly liked, but, in some way, they each admired.

Patricia said, "Victor knew how to get what his clients needed, I'll give him that. Somehow, some way, he made things happen that worked out, even for his worst client. They stayed with him over the years. He had a good reputation that way."

She avoided mentioning his reputation for other abilities that he had, such as stringing along three women at once without ever having to talk himself out of an embarrassing situation.

Genevieve Martínez-Higgins nodded. Clarke Higgins sighed and uttered, "So much potential. Hispanics can't afford to have their best men whittled away like this. It's a loss for the entire community."

Reymundo and Carmen Fernández looked at each other, and their eyes exchanged the message that Clarke was the biggest hypocrite they had ever known, but they let pass his presumptuousness in speaking for a "community" that he belonged to only by marriage.

Reymundo grabbed Patricia's hand and said, "If there's anything we can do, let us know. Just in case, you know. Delgado had his ways, God knows, but just the same, what a terrible tragedy. I can't imagine how this could have happened."

Patricia thought that if Reymundo's statement was true, he was about the only one in Denver who hadn't speculated on how Victor Delgado had met his maker.

Delgado's murder had been the subject of rampant guesswork by media types, community leaders, and anyone else who cared to voice an opinion. The known facts were few but obvious. The lawyer had surprised the burglar, and, then, the shooting. After that, anyone from hyper talk show hosts to sanctimonious op-ed writers for the Spanish language newspapers had come up with a theory about the why and the who.

A disgruntled client. A racist skinhead who wanted to strike a blow against a well-known and successful minority personality. A jealous husband. That one got Patricia's vote. Or, the most likely, Patricia had to admit, a careless burglar who didn't know enough to make sure that the office was empty before he crawled through the open bathroom window.

There was plenty of conjecture, and she knew that no matter what Reymundo said out loud, he and Carmen had their own version of the most notorious death that had taken place in years among this particular crowd of people. They were "professionals," and they thought lawyers, and others of similar ilk, should at least be immune to the violence, the blood and meaningless death that, on some days, made up a regular part of the routine in the neighborhoods surrounding the church. Those were the same neighborhoods where, on some days, the only professionals in sight were officers of la migra, cautiously going about their work.

■

Elías Garza tapped a thick cigar in a jade jaguar ashtray. He let out a large bellow of smoke that drifted up to whirling fan blades. He sighed every few minutes. Lately, it seemed, he wasted a lot of time waiting for Lorraine.

A skinny, tall man dressed in charcoal gray pants and a tan knit shirt rushed through the door. Perspiration beaded along a deep furrow in his forehead. He was alone.

"Santiago!" Garza shouted. "¿Qué pasa? What the hell is going on, man? Where is she?"

"Jefe, I . . . she's gone," the skinny man said. "She left last night. No one saw or heard her. That little slut, Frida, she must have helped her get out. The bitch drove into town to visit her sister. Mrs. Garza must have gone with her."

Elías Garza threw his cigar against the wall. Ashes

sprayed. The cigar smoldered in the carpet. Garza stretched his neck like a preening peacock. He glared at the man who one day expected to take over the operation in Ciudad Juárez.

"How many fucking men I got working for me here?" Garza bellowed. "Twenty, thirty? They got nothing to do all damn day except a few errands, check in people at the front gate, and watch those who want to leave. That's all! Nothing, they got nothing else to do! And they can't even do that!"

He knocked the ashtray off the table. It landed at Santiago's feet. The man flinched. He raised his hands, the palms facing Garza.

"Elías, hold on," Santiago pleaded. "We got the maid. Frida will tell us where she took Mrs. Garza. We'll go after her, bring her back."

"No shit, Santiago? You're really going to do all that?"

His eyes narrowed and stared through his lieutenant.

Santiago backed up a half step. That look had often been the precursor to someone's death. He waited for Garza to do something.

Garza almost whispered, "After Frida tells you everything she knows, finish it so that every other fucking donkey I got working around here gets the message. I want it to be a loud and clear message. You understand?"

Santiago nodded, then turned and ran from the room.

Garza poured amber liquid from a shiny chrome-plated decanter that rested on his desk. He took a long, slow drink. He crushed the still smoking cigar under his shoe. Now he did whisper.

"She didn't even say good-bye."

15

Before he had the power and money of old man Cardoza behind him, small things, such as a slip of the tongue or an eavesdropped telephone conversation, had caused Elías Garza grief and anxiety in quantities disproportionate to their size. He had developed a reluctance to talk on the telephone, and he used the machine only when he had convinced himself that it was absolutely essential. The disappearance of Lorraine was one of those times. He wanted to get the conversation over with as quickly as possible, but he had to make it clear to his man what he wanted.

"Lorraine ran away. It's been two days. She must be headed back up there."

The man they called Fidel smothered his surprise at hearing directly from Garza. He asked, "Why would she do that? It's not safe for her. She understands that."

Garza had to be patient. "She knows about the operation, all of it, from you and the others to all of the connections. Routes, drop-off points, deliverymen. All of it.
She's been a part of everything, and now she wants to use
that against me. She will need to get in touch with someone she thinks she can trust."

"Is it the money?"

Elías Garza laughed.

"Don't be naive. It's not good on you. She has money.
She wants revenge. For the agent."

The man on the other end of the line said nothing.
Revenge for Kiko Vigil eventually had to mean coming
after him.

Garza asked his man the question that only he could
answer. "Who will she think she can go to? I want her to
believe that she is safe. Then I will come up and take care
of it myself. Find the one she thinks is her ally and make
sure that he does what we need. Then let me know when
she's there."

Garza didn't wait for an answer. It was enough that he
had asked the question. He hung up the phone. He chewed
on the end of his cigar. He turned to Santiago Jiménez.

"Fly to Denver tonight. Keep your eye on our friend.
Call me when you know that Lorraine is in town or our
friend starts acting funny. If everything is the way it should
be, he will call me around the same time, with the same
message about Lorraine. If not, then you will be very busy.
Understand?"

Santiago said, "Yes, of course."

Garza slowly raised himself from his chair and just as
slowly walked over to his lieutenant. He stared at the

man who had been with him almost since the first day he had come to Mexico. He spoke with no hint of emotion in his voice.

"Nothing is 'of course,' Santiago. You made a big mistake by letting Lorraine get away. But you are my friend, my son's godfather. And you did take care of Vigil. You and Fidel. You brought her back to me. So, you have a second chance, something that no one else around here will ever have. It's all you will get, Santiago. Watch for her, let me know when she arrives, and then help me clean up this mess that you allowed to get this far. If you can do these things, then there is hope for you and the Juárez job. I don't have to tell you what will happen if you cannot do these things, do I?"

Again Garza didn't expect an answer to his question. Santiago avoided Garza's eyes and left the room.

Garza relit his cigar and gazed out the only window in the room. He stood there for several minutes until he saw the lights from the garage, then the headlights of Santiago's car as they flashed in an arc across the massive iron gate.

In Denver, the man who had been talking to Elías Garza had also spent several minutes in silence contemplating the implications of their conversation. He, too, stared out a window.

A full summer moon hung low over the horizon, framing the city skyline against the mountains. The beautiful Colorado summer night was wasted on the man.

Garza is scared, nervous about his whore and what she can do. He didn't even mention the unfinished Delgado problem. It is his own fault. He used to be in control. He used to be cold and strong. But she has taken that from him, made him a jealous man, and that means weakness. He let her get away! The Vigil killing—that could have been disastrous. Necessary only because of her. And now she's on the loose. I have to watch my ass, or the two of them will crush me in the middle.

He rolled a cold can of beer across his sweaty forehead.

Garza said to find the man that Lorraine would think of as her ally. He doesn't see it. She will come to me. That night they took her back to Mexico, she blamed Elías—it didn't matter what I did. She will assume that her special knowledge about me gives her an edge. She can hold on to that for as long as she wants. Until she believes that I'm ready to make a move against Elías Garza. Then I'll make the call, and the boss can finish it.

He didn't think it strange that he could tell himself what he was going to do while all the time, he knew that there was another play that he could make, and it would be so easy. Lorraine *would* trust him. She would want to take over the operation and bring him into it, with her.

He dredged up his favorite image of Lorraine Garza. She had just finished a shower when he had come by with a package of money from one of the deliveries. Wet hair, skin flushed from scrubbing and hot water. A towel uneasily clung to her torso. He couldn't escape the feeling that her appearance hadn't been an accident of timing. She allowed him to see her like that for a reason.

He had no doubt that he could run the business with Lorraine—he already took care of most of the details, and with her they could do it all. Or, better yet, without her, after he had from her everything he needed or wanted. He was a realist, and enough of a cynic to acknowledge the alternatives. Even if she only wanted to use him to get rid of Elías, even if she expected a payback for Kiko Vigil, then, that was okay, too. More than one could play that game. He only needed to get his hands on the controls, and then it would be simple. Bloody, maybe, but that couldn't be helped. That's the way the business was these days. Risky. Bloody. But so profitable.

First things first. He had to wrap up the Delgado part and deal with the loss of the tapes. Those could hurt Garza, maybe stop the entire operation. He had to prevent that, especially now that he had finally fashioned a plan, when it all seemed so clear to him. The memory of Lorraine Garza fresh out of a shower drifted back into his head. He drove to Danny Mora's office.

■

Tomás Chávez had fretted for most of the day about the last time he had seen Danny Mora. The argument, the sudden change in mood at the mention of the Compeáns, and the strange signals Danny had given out—Tomás couldn't understand any of it. He had called him and left a message, but there had been no return call. Danny had mumbled something about leaving town. Was he really gone? Rather than continue south to his new apartment, Chávez exited I-25 at Speer Boulevard North and, even though it was late, he headed for Danny's home.

The house was dark. He parked in the street in the same spot where he must have parked hundreds of times over the years. Danny's friendship had been one constant. A picture formed that had significance only for the two of them: *Chacho and Moony raced across Santa Fe Boulevard. Chacho slipped on loose gravel on the asphalt and fell to his knees. A twisted ankle kept Chacho down. Without missing a beat, Moony picked him up and carried him out of harm's way. A chorus of screechy brakes played in the background. Horns bleated. Curses flew at them like poison darts, and they laughed and taunted the drivers from the safety of the curb.* Chávez smiled. To hell with Moony's rudeness. Even Patricia had forgiven him. Moony had been one of the best things that had happened to him in his life. He had to talk with his old *compa.*

Chávez wondered what Danny could know about the Compeáns that would make him jumpy. It was probably nothing, he thought. *Danny always has been an intense guy. Hard to get to know, as they say.* He had started to pull away from the curb when . . . He swung his head at the gleam in the window that had caught the corner of his vision. The light moved through the room as though someone were carrying a candle. He quickly turned off the ignition. A figure crept through the house, and Chávez instinctively knew that it wasn't Danny.

He sneaked along the side of the house, near the short, squat bushes, until he came to a window that was half open. Should he climb in, wait for someone to leave, or get the cops? Danny could be in trouble. Moony knew some very dangerous people. If he was in there . . .

He looked around the yard. A stone about the size of a softball lay on the sparse lawn. His fingers gripped the stone as he stuck his head through the window and pulled himself through. He fell to his knees. The light had disappeared. Danny's home office was in the back of the house, across the room. He raised himself to a half crouch and moved toward the back.

A sound like a swish of cloth, like a draft of air had

116 •

ruffled a sheet hanging on a clothesline, stopped him. Chávez turned in the direction of the swish, but the darkness was so complete that he couldn't see anything other than shadows. He held his breath.

He wasn't alone in the room. There was a presence that seemed to suck up the air. He had made a mistake. Danny Mora wasn't in the house. He had to get out.

He squinted in a fruitless attempt to make out details, and as his eyes accustomed themselves to the lack of light, he satisfied himself that he was only a few feet from the front door. If he ran, he could make it to the outside before the intruder had a chance to react. If he stayed where he was, the intruder would zero in on him and get to him, where he was defenseless except for the useless stone that he still clutched.

He swallowed a deep breath of air. He ran the six or seven feet to the door. He heard the words, "What the . . ." behind him, then the steps of a hard-charging man. He grabbed the doorknob, turned it. Locked. He ducked and rolled to the side. A dull thump told him that the man had banged into the door. Chávez crawled for the open window. He shouted, "Help! Police! Help!"

The man jumped on him and smothered his mouth with a gloved hand. His other hand smashed into Tomás's side. The knife blade sliced through Tomás's ribs and into his lungs. His shouts were stopped, buried in his chest forever. Tomás slumped to the carpet, blood flowing from his side. He saw the man climb through the window. He wheezed, used his neck muscles to vainly pull in air. He closed his eyes and thought of Patricia Montelibre, then he thought of Lydia, then he thought of nothing.

■

Cruz Venegas struggled to keep his eyes on the ruts in the hard gravel. He had driven the route dozens of times, but he hadn't adapted to the feel of the new pickup, and he would never get used to the eerie desert night. The woman only made it worse. Sitting inches from her, he had trouble concentrating on the winding road—if it could be called a road—but he knew that he had to.

He had heard of other drivers who had been spooked by the sudden appearance of a coyote—the furry kind, not the human model of which Cruz himself was a damn good sample. Out of the darkness the red eyes of the four-footed scavengers would shine in the headlights and surprise the already jumpy smugglers, some of whom would twist the steering wheel and end up mired in sand past the axles of their trucks. If they didn't get the vehicle and its cargo free, they were easy targets for la migra, or wild dogs, or the more terrible animals who preyed on the lost, frightened, and weak in the Sonoran Desert.

Cruz knew the dangers, but his eyes insisted on finding the woman. Her outfit of jeans, an American-style western shirt, a suede jacket with fringe on the sleeves, and cowboy boots didn't appeal to him in any special way, but with her sitting next to him in the cab of the pickup truck, he couldn't calm his urges. Not many women traveled with him in the front seat across the deserted back roads and almost invisible trails that he had to use under cover of darkness. She was special, in many ways.

He had picked her up in Sonoita on the Mexican side of the border. His *cuñado,* Hermán, had passed her along to him with a big gold-toothed grin and a message.

"She's important. Gallegos said to make sure that she makes it to Phoenix. There's a extra four hundred gringo dollars for you when you get back."

He brought her across the border without incident— that was his basic job, and he did it well. Because of Hermán's concern, he allowed her to ride with him, away from the elbow-to-elbow and butt-to-butt cramped quarters in the specially designed camper shell over the back of the new but very dusty truck. She knew more about the route than he did, and he guessed that she must have made the trip many times before. Her importance had to mean that she was related to someone, and that usually meant hands off, but still, they were alone as far as anyone who mattered was concerned—the *mojados* didn't count for anything—and what he had seen of her convinced him that she might be worth the risk.

Gallegos was one of the main guys in the Julio Díaz outfit, out of San Luis Potosí, and Cruz Venegas had heard the stories about the Díaz and Cardoza-Garza rivalry. The boys were locked in a bloody little war. Why, then, had Gallegos been the one to set up her trip? She probably had something to do with the war. His *pendejo* brother-in-law might have got him into something that he didn't really want any part of. The Cardoza-Garza *asesinos* were cold-blooded torturers and more. He had heard enough late night tall tales about the bodies of other drivers, coyotes like him, found in a dozen pieces strewn along the highway to warn off the competition. He shuddered and drew his thin jacket closer around his chest. He stared even harder at the beam of his headlights in an attempt to ward off the evil thoughts that had chilled his bones.

Lorraine Garza felt for the grip of her handgun. It rested against her hip, tight in the waist of her jeans and hidden by her jacket. So far, she hadn't needed it. Pedro Gallegos had been almost too easy, she thought. He had slobbered over her, literally rubbed his greasy palms together when he finally understood that she was offering him a chance to do something that could hurt Elías Garza.

He could have caused her pain, but when he saw the bruises on her face and the puffed eye and listened to her tear-filled explanation of all that had gone bad between her and Elías, Gallegos knew that hurting her, even killing her, wouldn't mean much to his rival. She wanted to get back to the States, back to where she had spent several years running Garza's operation, and she promised him a piece of whatever action she could take over. He only half believed her, but the important thing was helping her simply so that Garza would know that it had been done and that he, Pedro Gallegos, had been the man who had slipped the woman out of Mexico right under the noses of Garza's men. Gallegos intended to have it all, with or without Lorraine Garza's cooperation. Helping her escape and letting her return to Colorado might pay off one day, or she just might end up dead. Either way, Pedro Gallegos thought he couldn't lose.

He left the details to Hermán Saucedo, a good man who would make sure that she crossed the border safely and then have someone ready to take her farther north. For a thousand dollars a head, Hermán Saucedo was the best there was at sneaking contraband of all types into the United States of America. And because Hermán also was a good businessman and his experience alerted him to the

delicate nature of the woman's journey, he had only doubled his usual price.

She had become incredibly tired over the past few
hours, and it had taken a supreme act of will to remain
awake. She hadn't really slept in more than forty-eight
hours. She didn't trust Venegas, but then, what was there
to trust? He was a pock-marked, overweight man who kept
his hair long. It flopped across his shoulders in a dusty
ponytail. He made a living by running people and drugs
across the border, and he had no doubt killed a few in the
course of earning that living. Still, she was so tired . . .

The truck veered to the left and stopped abruptly. The
human freight rolled from side to side. They were unable
to brace themselves. They shouted in the darkness.

Lorraine jerked awake and pulled the gun from her
pants. Something was happening. It could be Venegas, it
could be la migra, it could be a gang of bandits. She looked
at Venegas. His eyes were wide in terror.

He shouted at her, "Run! They blocked the road. Try
to—"

The window near his head shattered and blood
smeared the inside of the cab. Something wet and warm
sprayed her face. Venegas slumped to his right. His head
gushed blood over the cheap upholstery. She screamed and
pushed open the truck's door and fell to the dirt. Men and
women were scrambling from the back of the truck. There
were more shots, screams, curses. The bright moon gave
her enough light to run to a ridge only a few yards from
the pickup. Several men shouted in Spanish.

"¡Alto! ¡No corran!"

"¡Sólo queremos dinero!"

"¡No los vamos a lastimar!"

She ignored their shouts to stop running, that they only wanted money, and that they wouldn't hurt her. She heard others running, too. More shots, more screams. She ran uphill, trying to keep her profile as low as she could.

Someone grabbed her arm and yanked her to the ground. She smelled liquor and cigarette smoke and days of caked sweat. The man shoved himself on her and ripped at her jeans. She looked into his eyes but saw nothing except the gleam of the pickup truck's headlights. She and the man wrestled on the ground.

She wrenched her arms free and clawed at his face, and then she felt the earth give way. They fell over the short ridge, and the man lost his hold on her. She hit the dirt with a soft thud of her backside, but the man's face smashed against the earth. He rolled on his back, and she saw that he was having trouble catching his breath. The fall had knocked the air out of his lungs.

She put the gun to his head. The dull, unseeing eyes now reflected fear. She pulled the trigger and scarcely noticed the noise or the jerk of her hand. The man's head viciously snapped with the force of the bullet.

She crawled to the top of the ridge and fell into a thicket of bushes. She lay panting in the darkness.

A group of men surrounded the pickup. One of them pulled Venegas's body from the cab. A series of gunshots exploded as the body was riddled with bullets. More men appeared, and they brought with them some of the unlucky men and women who had been in the back of the truck. They were all searched and their meager possessions—wallets, rosaries, belts—were taken by the bandits. The women were stripped of their clothes, and three or four of the men took their turns with the younger ones. Two men wearing flannel shirts and straw hats tried to stop the rapes. They were shot immediately. The other men were all beaten. A young man, who appeared to be a teenager, was dragged from the group by the men who were doing the raping. They pushed him from one to the other in a perverted game of catch, taking turns beating him in the face, then two of the bandits jumped him and tore off his clothes and raped him. The boy screamed, the women cried, the bandits laughed and cursed.

Lorraine Garza closed her eyes in terror, but she didn't allow screams and whimpers to escape her tightly clenched mouth. Her hands clutched the gun. The feel of the gun was the only hard piece of reality that she allowed to enter her mind during the insanity of the night. She hadn't released it by the time the sun rose.

She was alone in the desert. The bandits had slithered back to the rocks where they had come from, and their dazed, injured victims had gathered together and wandered into the heat of the desert, heading in a general northerly direction.

She had survived the night.

16

Santiago Jiménez impatiently waited for the man he knew only as Fidel. North Americans, he thought, have too much time on their hands. Dressed in a green golf shirt, lightweight summer slacks, and a pair of soft shoes that the gringo salesman had called "city sandals," he sat in a place that served bagels, coffee, and herb tea. His view included several tall buildings and constantly moving small groups of people.

Is it possible that they all have out-of-the office meetings or midmorning coffee breaks to which they can leisurely stroll? The tourists, yes, understandable. A beautiful city, money to throw away on assorted trinkets and junk. A day inside the tall buildings would be wasted when the sunshine and blue sky beckon so invitingly. This city is nothing like Mexico City, where the sky stays hidden for days and where walking the hazy, dirt-clogged streets results only in a rough, scratchy throat and fits of coughing.

Fidel entered the coffee shop and, without ordering anything from the boy behind the counter, sat in the empty chair across from Santiago.

Santiago nodded. He had many things to say. Where should he begin?

"Kiko Vigil drags me back to your city. I thought we had solved that problem. But the woman . . ."

Fidel stared.

"This latest incident is not good," Jiménez continued. "Elías is very unhappy that yet another man with a high visibility has become associated with our affairs. Why is this happening?"

Fidel's eyes shrank as though a bright light had exploded over his pupils. An emptiness flooded his face. He answered in crisp, precise Spanish.

"Bad luck, that's all. The first, the lawyer, had to be removed, that was what I understood Elías wanted. The lawyer, like all lawyers, was greedy. He was threatening to do something crazy with the information he had about the operation, something like go to the police. He knew all about the business here, and he had vital knowledge about many of us. I was ordered to remove the threat of that knowledge. The lawyer was removed. The files on the work that he did for us were not in the office. Neither were the tapes. I know that an investigator also had an interest in this information. I am not sure why. I searched the investigator's office—nothing."

Santiago nodded and asked, "But you didn't find our information in the house, either?"

"No." Fidel shrugged as though that was enough of an explanation. "The investigator left town, and no one should have been at his house. The writer was a surprise and in the way. I had no choice. But I couldn't take the time to really look. Tell Elías that I will fix this. I plan to try again."

Santiago had a mild curiosity about a man who would profess to be an "investigator." It was an unusual, archaic thing to do with one's life. He asked another question.

"What do you know about this investigator?"

"His name's Daniel Mora. He worked for the lawyer a few years back. He has a very good reputation for what he does, but there is something about him that puts people off—cold, maybe too much of a tough guy, you know what I mean?"

Fidel smiled broadly, but Santiago was not amused.

Fidel shrugged again. He had heard from others in the organization that Santiago was a prick, and now he believed it. They had worked well together that night they had taken out Vigil, but that was old news. Things had changed.

"Maybe the lawyer gave the investigator the tapes for safekeeping. Maybe Mora was still dealing with some aspect of the work for the lawyer. I don't know. But I plan to get the information, in whatever way I have to. That's always been my plan."

Santiago shook his head. He fingered one of the specially made cigars that Elías had given him before Lorraine had escaped.

"No. There will be no more surprises. If we have to kill Mora, then it will be done when we want it done, in a professional way. It should not be a situation again of someone showing up where you did not expect them to be. Damn you, Fidel, you were sloppy, careless. And we have more important problems now. Put that job on the back burner. The priority is Lorraine Garza. She is far more of a threat than anything this investigator can do with the lawyer's files. She must be coming back to Denver. Elías wants you to find her and watch her or, better yet, win her confidence. When she's set up, Elías will take over. Is that understood?"

Fidel squinted at the man who had called him sloppy and careless. They owed him so much, he shouldn't have to put up with rudeness.

"Yes. I already knew that. You didn't have to tell me again. I can take care of my job. I have for years, and I will continue to do so. Tell Elías it's all under control."

He had to get away from the man from Mexico City. He could feel the anger growing in his guts, and that would do him no good. He looked around the shop, from the last booth to the front door, then left without another word to Santiago Jiménez.

Santiago pulled a thin black lighter from the shirt pocket over his heart. He lit the cigar and was drawing comfortably on the smoke when the boy behind the counter caught his attention with an angry wave.

"It's nonsmoking."

The boy pointed at a sign on the wall that had a red slash through a drawing of a lit cigarette. Santiago frowned, continued puffing on the cigar, and slowly walked out of the shop.

■

"I can't do anything. I can't seem to go on. I have to know why Tomás was killed. His friend, Danny, he knows something, he has to, and I have to talk to him. I have to know."

Patricia Montelibre had finally quit crying. Silvia

poured another cup of coffee for her grieving friend. Patricia had moved in with Silvia since Tomás's funeral; she couldn't be alone. She had no one other than Silvia to talk with; no one else cared what the mistress, the short-time girlfriend, felt or suffered. She had convinced herself that she had to get together with Danny Mora.

Silvia held her friend's hand.

"Don't do this. You have to let it go. It was a break-in, a burglary that Tomás stumbled across, just like Victor Delgado. Nobody could have done anything about it. Tomás saw a light in the house when he knew his friend wasn't home. He stopped to check it out, and the thief . . ."

Patricia avoided looking at her friend. It was too easy for Silvia. Almost everything was.

"Yes, yes, you're right, of course. But I still have to talk with Danny. You know, they argued the last time they saw each other. Maybe he wants to talk with me, too."

Silvia rubbed Patricia's hand. Patricia drew back from her friend.

Silvia acted as though her friend hadn't pulled away. She said, "If that were true, don't you think he would have called you by now? And anyway, I can't say I like that man. Something about him. Leave him alone. It must be terrible for him, too. It was his house. They were friends since they were boys, long before you . . ."

Again Silvia didn't finish her thought.

"Right, long before Tomás and I were together. Don't you think I know that? Danny and Tomás were so close, maybe talking with Danny is just another way of trying to hang on to Tomás. Damn it, I don't know. I just have to see him."

Silvia cringed. There was something almost desperate

about her friend's state of mind. She would have to watch her closely, go with her if she followed through on trying to see Danny Mora. Mora—that man again. Charles had used him, and now Patricia needed him. Tragedy followed him like the moon followed the sun. What was it about Danny Mora that attracted the darkness?

Silvia resolved to talk it over with Charles. At least he was good for that.

■

Daniel Mora's patience served him well during the time of Tomás Chávez's funeral. Mora assumed the role of the eldest brother in the Chávez family. He made the arrangements, notified those who needed to know, organized the events that had to be part of the mourning process, and consoled those who wanted that. He was the right man to talk with Tomás's mother when she had to hear how much the loss of Tomás meant to everyone who knew him. Through it all he maintained a respectful dignity that honored Tomás and his memory.

Only Lydia was inconsolable. No one, including Danny Mora, could calm her down.

Patricia Montelibre wanted to talk with him, but she couldn't bring herself to make the effort, not that day, not with the people who filled Our Lady of Guadalupe. Lydia and Tomás's relatives hovered around Danny, and so she avoided him. Silvia Compeán stayed at her side and, together, they were ignored by all the other mourners. Patricia stayed in the background, keeping her grief to herself. She left before the services were over.

Only when he was alone, hours after the last person

had expressed their sorrow and gratitude for everything he had done for the family, did Danny Mora allow the thoughts he had held at bay to overtake him.

The house technically still was a crime scene, and police tape ringed the perimeter of his yard. Someone had cleaned up the place where Tomás had died, he wasn't sure who, but he hadn't stayed in his home since he had returned from Texas. The day of the funeral he checked out of the cheap motel and decided that the time had come for him to resume his own routines, his own life. But he found that impossible. He made his way home from his downtown office late, after ten. Sleep was out of the question. He tried a shot of the whiskey he kept in the cupboard, but he didn't relax. He couldn't rest in the house where Tomás had died, and there was no one for him to call. He felt feverish, and his teeth ached because he had clenched his jaws since he had learned of Tomás's death.

Out of frustration with himself more than anything else, he climbed on his bike, and through the night he raced to the trail he had ridden so many other times, but this time it was without any feeling of elation or even exertion. His legs ground out the miles on his private road to hell in darkness and self-pity. He tried to make the winding path along the South Platte River his route to escape, his midnight express away from Tomás's death, but it didn't work.

Streetlights, passing traffic, and the reflections from the downtown buildings provided the illumination he needed to stay on the trail. There was no moon to help. Trees, bushes, and a waist-high cement wall that appeared occasionally along the path created sharp, angular shadows. Where the trail paralleled I-25, the noise of night traffic echoed along the riverbank, making him feel more alone. He surprised drunks and homeless men as he sped by their temporary respites, oblivious to their taunts and curses, unmindful of the ubiquitous danger. A black log in the path changed into the body of a man, sleeping, or passed out, or dead, he didn't know and he didn't stop to find out.

Sweat covered his face, and a few times he rode off the trail into the brush, where he crashed in a painful heap.

He rode on, beneath the ominous Public Service Company smokestacks that stood guard over the river. His legs pumped him past the Sun Valley Community Building and remodeled housing projects. He had become a piece of the machinery. He raced under the Mississippi Avenue bridge without realizing it. Thirty minutes into his ride, a sharp twinge crept up his calf, and his right leg stiffened. Weeds and bushes slapped at his ankles. At Overland Pond, his leg cramped completely, and he grunted with pain. He swerved into a grassy area. He lost control of the bike. His right leg refused to help him. With an effort made frantic by the onrushing darkness, he jumped off the bike and let it crash against a concrete bench, where it lay twisted in a question mark.

He rolled in the grass, then pulled himself to his knees. His leg throbbed, and he considered lying on his back. He raised himself at the waist. He retched, and his back jerked with spasms. Something bitter and warm crawled from his stomach and poured out of his mouth. He felt intoxicated, dizzy, and weak. His breath came in rapid bursts. He held his head in his hands.

Tomás stared at him in the darkness. His pain, his agony, seeped around the soul of Danny Mora. The blood that flowed onto the wooden floor of Danny Mora's house pumped from Danny Mora's heart. Tomás's terror doubled up Danny Mora. Danny Mora's brain struggled for an answer, grasped for any clue, any sign, any small piece of understanding. Danny Mora cried in the night, alone.

17

A yellow-and-green forked tongue curved lasciviously along the jaw of a purple, almost black creature with pointed, hairy ears that stood at rapt attention, anticipating a sound that might mean dinner or companionship—the creature's leer could mean either, Patricia had decided. The ceremonial mask came from deep in central Mexico, and that was all she knew about Mora's collection.

After several telephone messages, he had agreed to meet her at his office. He had shown her to the chair in his main room, then disappeared with the statement that he would return in a few minutes. She had waited fifteen, and still no Danny Mora.

His office had surprised her. The masks, the huge, obviously old wooden table, and the general neatness were unexpected. She admitted to herself that she had not known what to expect. Mora had been an enigma since she had first met him, and the objects in his office added nothing to any potential solution. The odd masks certainly spoke to his awareness of his cultural and ethnic roots, but why so many, and why so many that hinted at dark rituals in frenzied tropical nights? The sweet aroma of mesquite hung in the air; the fecund scent of wet earth emanated from the heavy table. For such a large piece of furniture, the desk held few papers and only one file folder. The office was immaculate, so tidy that she unconsciously smoothed the wrinkles on her blouse sleeves.

Silvia had argued against her having anything to do with Mora, she had called him "a man of trouble," but Patricia knew that if there were any answers for what had happened to Tomás, Danny Mora was the person who would have them. She had made the appointment without telling Silvia. Her friend thought she was visiting her own family, taking time to get back to the people who could help her get over Tomás.

When he finally appeared, he carried several expandable envelopes of papers and a plastic box filled with cassette tapes. He said, "Sorry about the wait. When you called, I tried to organize this stuff. I had a mess in here, but I think I got it together again. Here it is."

Patricia thanked him for seeing her. "It means a lot that you'll talk with me."

He quickly nodded, then launched into his theory of what had happened to Tomás.

"The killer was searching my home for something that he couldn't find at my office. He was very careful, and I wouldn't have thought to check my office if hadn't been for what happened to Tomás, but there are signs that someone rifled my file cabinets, picked through my desk, and so on. After he had no luck here, he must have gone to my house, where Tomás surprised him. The killer had to leave in a hurry after Tomás showed up, obviously, so he didn't finish his search. He didn't bother to put anything away; with Tomás's body there was no reason to hide the fact that someone had broken into my house. I'm convinced that the killer was looking for this stuff. It's been here, in my office, until I left town. I looked at the files one more time the night we all got together at Tomás's house, and then I put all of this in a safe I have at my house." He paused, then added, "The safe is hidden in the garage, where I keep my bike. Someone would need a lot of time to find it and then open it."

Patricia tried to take in everything he said, but she stopped him to give her time to put it together.

"In a safe?" she asked. "Why? Did you know someone was looking for these files? Did you know someone might kill for these papers?"

"The killing of Victor Delgado made me wary. The timing was too coincidental. These files and tapes came from Delgado. I took them from him only a few days before he was killed."

Her eyes flared. She blurted, "And Tomás was killed in the same way as Victor—a surprised intruder. Someone looking for something at Victor's office, then at your office, finally, your house. There has to be a connection."

He looked directly at her. The oval face and strong chin mirrored the photos he had seen over the years of her brother, Carlos. "Yes, I think so. Of course, there is one other connection, one even more obvious."

She wrinkled her brow and waited for him to continue. What could it be? What was so obvious?

She bolted from her chair.

"It's me! From Victor Delgado to Tomás Chávez. And now they're both dead."

"Yes." He tried to be low-key. "You and your affairs with these men. There is that. There could be a jealous lover of yours who intends to eliminate all rivals. You should tell me about that if it's true, if you think it's possible."

"There's no one like that." She shook her head. "No one that crazy. No one who could . . ."

"I didn't really think so. You need to watch for any sign that it could be someone like that—someone following you, or maybe only a feeling you get. Let me know immediately if you sense anything. Okay?"

"Yes. Of course. But that's not what you expect, is it?"

"No. You should be careful, but the answer is in these files, and what they hold about a man neither one of us knows. A man who has taken someone from both of us."

She picked up one of the file folders and leafed through several of its pages.

"Elías Garza? A Mexican gangster? That's who killed Tomás? Tomás would never have been involved with such a man."

She handed him the file, and he placed it on the top of the stack. He said, "It wasn't Garza directly. He seldom does his own dirty work. Had to be someone working for him. And it has nothing to do with Tomás."

She wanted to understand, but it made no sense to her. "What could be so important about Victor's files that he and

Tomás were killed? What could possibly be in these papers that meant Tomás had to die, that . . ."

She faltered, and the emotion of talking about Tomás threatened to overwhelm her. She murmured incoherent words.

"Papers! Goddamn papers!"

For several minutes silent sobs wrenched her shoulders and back. She turned away and tried to regain control. When she could talk again, she said, "I'm sorry."

He said, "It's all right. The same thing happens to me."

She dug out a tissue from a pocket of her dress and blew her nose. He said, "I've looked through these pages a hundred times. I've listened to these tapes until I know them by heart. I've seen some things that help me with my job, heard Garza confess to crimes that should get him executed, but nothing that isn't known or suspected by the cops. In other words, no smoking gun. Nothing that Tomás had to die for."

Danny Mora stared at pages from one of the files, picking his words. He was careful with Patricia.

"I don't know for sure, of course. Victor probably wanted money, a payoff for keeping quiet about what he had learned from representing Garza. Or Garza just got nervous. He wanted the files and tapes secured, safe. No more loose ends. Elías Garza is a man who doesn't like loose ends, especially about his business. The files and tapes are just that—loose ends that he wants back. And people are dying for that."

Patricia moved closer to Danny. She said, "Victor was killed because this . . . killer was looking for these things at Victor's office. He didn't know about you; he wasn't really trying to stop whatever it is you're doing. This started before that, or, at least, before anyone knew about your role. The killer would have gone to your place first instead of wasting time at Victor's office. He must have learned that you had the tapes after that, after Victor's death, and then he went to your office, and then your house, where . . ."

"Right. But Victor wasn't just an unlucky sap. Maybe the poor sonofabitch rubbed Garza the wrong way. Maybe he wanted more legal fees than Garza thought he should have to pay. Maybe Delgado just played it stupid."

She cringed at his unsentimental dismissal of Victor, but she didn't say anything.

"Anyway, Delgado gets his, the tapes aren't found, the killer concludes I've got something he might want, maybe from something Victor said before he killed him. Then he waits until I'm out of town, doesn't find anything at my office, tries my house. Tomás, unlike Delgado, is innocent of anything that could be a reason for all of this. It's the scenario that makes the most sense. Or the least, depending on how you look at it."

Patricia said, "It's so meaningless, so sad." She said what had nagged at her since he had begun his explanation. "You're the one in danger now. Tomás was simply in the way, but you . . . You have these tapes and all of Victor's notes about Garza. Have you gone to the police? They should arrest Garza."

Now he moved closer to her. He shook his head.

"Garza's untouchable. The police would need more than my speculations about him to even try to get him to respond. And I doubt any district attorney could rely on these tapes alone to prosecute a high-profile defendant like Garza. Going after Garza is a waste of time. I have to find the killer him-self, the man working for Garza, the man whose job is to find these." He pointed at the files and cassettes.

"That man knows about you," she insisted. "He's already killed two men; he won't hesitate to kill you, too. You have to go to the police."

"It won't do any good. Take my word on that."

His finality bothered her. She said, "I could conclude that you are a very stubborn man. Or that there's more. Something to do with your own needs. Your personal stake in all this."

He said nothing. She moved on. "If you're not going to the police, what, then? How do you plan to find this man, this murderer?"

Again he didn't answer. She asked another question. "What could you be working on that has to do with Garza?"

For Tomás, he gave her what he thought he should.

"I was hired to learn what I could about another man that Garza ordered murdered, a federal agent. You might remember it, the shooting of Francisco Vigil at a downtown bar. One of Vigil's friends didn't like it that no one was ever prosecuted for the murder or that his friend's record was blemished because of the circumstances of the killing. It's pretty clear that Garza had the agent shot, but again, no one can touch him."

"If the police couldn't get to Garza, what are you being paid to do?"

"My job is to answer some questions for the friend, clean the slate, so to speak. It has more to do with reputa-tion than anything else, if you can believe that."

The sadness had returned, but she didn't break down.

She remained silent while Mora told her more about what he thought had to be done. He finally responded to her unanswered questions.

While he talked, the evening sun settled behind the distant mountains, and the room dimmed. Danny Mora stood half in darkness, an eerie, stoic statue that gave nothing away. Shadows from the windowpanes crisscrossed the masks on the wall, and, from deep within herself, she sensed that everything had changed.

18

The apartment manager remembered the dark-haired, attractive Mexican woman with the heavy accent. He didn't hesitate to re-rent to her, especially as the apartment had been vacant for weeks and she wanted to pay rent several months in advance. She looked worn out, and her clothes needed a good cleaning, but she had the money and she still had that same way about her, that attitude that he recalled from many months before when she and her man had made regular visits to the buffet apartment.

Nothing had changed. The same mass-produced, cheaply framed print of watercolor tulips hung crookedly on the wall, same shabby throw rug on the scratched and squeaky wooden floor, same sofa bed with the sagging mattress. It had served Lorraine and Kiko well—their place for laughter, promises, and love.

No one connected to Elías had any clue about their hideaway. She had made sure of that, and it was the only spot in all of Denver that she could return to and feel somewhat safe.

Lorraine struggled out of her ruined shirt, unclasped her bra and let it fall to the floor, and searched the three rooms for a towel. She found a clean washcloth in a drawer in the kitchen, then used the towel and water from the bathroom sink to scrub her face, rinse off her torso, and soothe her skin.

Elías called this a whore's bath, un baño de puta.

She would shower later. After she had a chance to think.

She unfolded the sofa and stretched out on the lumpy bedding. She thought about Kiko. It seemed so long ago that he had held her in this room, so many lifetimes ago.

She was exhausted from her escape from Garza, but she had no time for rest. The nightmare journey from Mexico had deprived her of sleep and food. Her back ached, her skin was dry and parched, and when she touched her hair, a thin, oily film stuck to her fingers. She placed her palm on her warm forehead. She might have a fever.

After leaving the wrecked pickup, she tramped through the scorching desert, convinced that she would die. She didn't believe that she would survive until she stumbled over a cactus-covered rise and saw a highway cutting through the silvery haze. She caught several different rides with worried tourists and lecherous truckers. She begged for food. She sought out others like her in the alleys and back streets of the small towns along the highway. Men and women who were in the country illegally assumed she was one of them, and they gave her what they could. Vending machine bags of stale peanuts, cans of diet soda, a baloney sandwich. Men with rough hands and bloodred eyes offered full dinners, a soft bed, a warm shower, but she wasn't willing to pay their asking price.

Finally, days later, at an ATM in Grants, New Mexico, she retrieved enough money from one of the accounts that Garza didn't know about to buy a cheap used car. She drove away from the regular routes, through towns where she knew no one and, she hoped, no one recognized her.

She aimed for Denver, back to where it had all begun for her and back to where she hoped to end it. Somehow, some way, Elías would pay for Kiko.

Her first step would mean taking a risk, a gamble that could backfire and end it. She saw no other choice. She needed help. She had to make a move that might cost her everything, but she knew the man to call—a man with so much ambition that turning on Elías might sound like the natural thing for him to do. A man who would have no qualms about working with a woman who knew he had killed her lover.

She silently said a prayer to the Virgen de Guadalupe.

Holy Mother, you watched your son die, you helped Him in his hour of greatest need. Help me, please. With all the mercy in your sacred heart, with all the goodness you share with sinners and saints, help me with this terrible thing I must do. Help me, and I am yours, forever.

She picked up the phone, doubted herself, told herself no, not Kiko's killer, and finally, desperately, she punched in Fidel's number.

■

Silvia Compeán, Charles Compeán, Genevieve Martínez-Higgins, Clarke Higgins, Carmen Fernández, and Reymundo

Fernández had thoroughly enjoyed the band from Cuba. They'd had some problems understanding the fast Cuban Spanish from the bandleader as he had introduced the songs and the members of the group, but other than that minor irritation, the evening had been one of the best since all the trouble had begun. *Trouble* had become their word for the still unsolved deaths of Victor Delgado and Tomás Chávez. The old friends had decided to get past the trouble by spending a night together as they once had: dancing, partying, acting giddy and silly as though their youth and credit cards would last forever.

They had a great dinner of *pollo de la brasa, pescado al mojo de ajo,* and Peruvian Chinese noodles at Los Cabos II and then continued the party at another club on the downtown mall. They listened and danced to Los Van-Van, the visitors from Castro's island. The band had made them sweat and holler with fiery, sensuous rhythms that blended a Caribbean beat, New York City rap, African passion, and the down-and-dirty movements of lusty, sexual women and men who wanted only to have a good time.

After the last encore, the last merengue, and the final call for drinks, they had retreated to an all-night diner on Colfax Avenue, a few blocks from the club, for some breakfast, coffee, and anticipated conversation.

Silvia's friends looked old and tired, but she shrugged off the implication for herself. The harsh, white glare of the diner and the earlier exertions on the dance floor had taxed the group, made them regret their inflexible bones and unused muscles. The women had objected to extending the night, but Clarke Higgins had insisted.

"Come on, viejas, don't act your age. We used to go out

all the time for breakfast after we finished with the clubs. We can still do it!"

And at first, the group had been animated at the restaurant, still running on the fumes from the nightclub and the frenzied music. They had talked for several minutes about everything from Hispanic Chamber of Commerce business to city politics to Latino movie stars.

In the middle of the conversation, Reymundo tapped Silvia on the shoulder.

"Tell me. Your friend, Patricia. How is she? Losing Chávez like that, so soon after Victor Delgado. Is she all right?"

These questions had been on the minds of the others, in one form or another, and they waited for Silvia to answer. Clarke and Genevieve politely picked at their food, Carmen sipped on watery orange juice, Charles cleared his throat and stared through a streaked window at the almost deserted street.

Silvia put down her fork, wiped her lips with a napkin. "Patricia seems to be doing well, thank you. Although to tell you the truth, it's been a few days since we've talked. She returned to her house, you know. Thought it was time, I guess."

Genevieve's thick eyebrows squeezed together at the middle of her forehead. "Really? I thought she would stay with you longer, a few weeks at least. Any news from the police? Anything happening with that?"

Silvia shrugged. "There must be—at least that's what Patty hinted at. She acted as though there was something, but she wouldn't say. Very tight-lipped, you know."

They looked at her and waited. There had to be more. They had never known Silvia Compeán to fail to find out the juiciest detail of the latest bit of gossip. They had no reason to expect the situation with her friend Patricia Montelibre to be any different. Silvia waited for a few heartbeats. She, too, knew what was expected.

"Patty's been acting strange lately. That damn girl. She did something that I didn't like, and I told her about it. I guess we had an . . . an argument. We were both upset when she left."

Charles sighed, nodded in agreement. He already missed Patricia Montelibre—so vibrant compared to the people sharing his booth.

He interjected, "Upset is a good way to put it. Silvia told Patricia that she should stay away from that friend of Chávez's, the detective, and Patricia didn't like it. I was surprised, I'll tell you. Patricia is usually so levelheaded. I think the trouble has all been too much of a strain. Can you believe, she told Silvia that she and this Mora guy are trying to find out who the killer is. Oh, that's right, they think Delgado and Chávez's deaths are connected, that there is only one murderer. I haven't heard that, and I don't think the police are looking at it that way. But that's what she said, right, Sil?"

Silvia clucked her tongue against her teeth, then answered, "I told her she was crazy. *Loca.* Well, isn't she? Does she really think that she can do anything about what happened to Tomás? And this guy—Danny Mora? Have any of you met him? He's spooky. Hanging around that guy is dangerous, could cause Patty trouble. But—she doesn't want to listen to me. She said he was on to something, but she wouldn't tell me more. Charles is right. *Es la verdad.* The strain of losing Victor and Tomás in a matter of a few days has affected her. What she really needs is someone to take her mind off what's happened, a fun guy, for a date, you know? Not this detective fellow that's only going to keep her all stirred up about this stuff. But like I said, she doesn't listen to me anymore."

The group had to agree with her, they always did, although no one said anything about it. They were drained from the night, and not one of them could imagine Patricia Montelibre associating with a private detective, especially not one whom everyone agreed came off as sinister and unfriendly. What could Patricia be thinking?

Staring at her runny, greasy eggs and toast soaked in butter, Silvia wanted only to go home and get some sleep. The conversation drifted away from her, and she lost interest. She felt herself nodding off, sliding down the slippery vinyl of the booth, when something Clarke Higgins said brought her back and made her sit up.

"Look, people, before you all leave. I wanted to show you something. Something new that I, uh, I've been saving for a special occasion. And now we have one. All of us, back together again, like the old days."

The group waited. There was no way to anticipate what Higgins was about to show them. He had surprised them in the past with so many off-the-wall antics that anything was possible. He removed his jacket, loosened his tie, and rolled up the left sleeve of his white shirt, stained at the cuffs and the neck and otherwise very wrinkled from the dancing. He exposed his upper arm, and there it was: a four-inch portrait of Emiliano Zapata, etched in dark blue. The dour Mexican revolutionary stared emptily from Higgins's wan, blotchy skin. He had a full, bushy mustache, bandoleers crossed his chest, and a wide sombrero shielded his famous eyes.

Genevieve Martínez-Higgins couldn't speak. She placed her hands at the front of her skull and slowly, tightly ran her fingers through her hair, as though she wanted to tear out the roots and drag out her brain so that she would have an excuse for not participating in the scene that was unfolding around her. She clenched her jaws and gradually bowed her head until it rested on the table.

Silvia started to laugh, then caught herself when Clarke's pained expression told her that he didn't see any humor in what he had done.

Reymundo Fernández and Charles Compeán avoided each other's eyes. They stared at the tattoo and tried to find words for what they thought they should say to the professor, who, apparently, had gone over the deep, deep end of cultural appropriation.

"Wow. When did you do that?"

Charles didn't really care when Clarke had submitted himself to the tattoo artist's needle, but it was all he could think of to try to ease the embarrassment they were feeling.

"A couple of days ago. I was at your place, and I saw that poster that Silvia has mounted in your basement. I've always admired it. It's a really terrific piece of art. So emotional, so sincere, you know? Anyway, I picked up another copy of the poster at Carmen and Rey's shop, took it down to Jorge at Tattoos-4-You, and here it is."

Carmen said, "If I had known that's what you wanted that poster for, I'm not sure I would have sold it to you, Clarke. A tattoo! My God! How could you have let him do that, Gen? Gen? Uh-oh. Clarke, you did talk it over with Genevieve before you did it, didn't you?"

Reymundo tapped his knee against Carmen's leg in an attempt to signal her that she should shut up, but it was too late.

Genevieve looked up from the table. "Hell, no, he didn't talk it over with me! This is the first I know about this. No wonder I saw bandages in the trash. He tried to tell me he cut himself at the gym. It was this damn thing—I hope it hurt like hell, Clarke."

Clarke Higgins didn't understand the reaction. He thought his friends would value what he had done. Zapata was an icon to them all. At least, that was what they said. And a tattoo—it was almost cultural, almost traditional for Chicanos to have a tattoo. Why couldn't he have one? What was wrong with these people?

"Well, I don't get it. If you don't like this one, then I guess you won't like . . ."

Genevieve didn't want to hear Clarke's unfinished sentence, but she asked anyway, in spite of her growing sense of nausea.

"What? What the hell else did you do, Clarke? What other stupid, *pendejada* did you do?"

Clarke looked around the table, took a drink of coffee, then shrugged. He started to roll up the sleeve on his right arm.

"Pancho Villa has always been one of my favorite heroes. How could I have Zapata without Villa?"

19

Eugene Nieto looked good in civilian clothes. Born to style! The department patrol uniform was too restrictive, too bland for such a good-looking guy as Clean Gene Nieto. Loved being a cop, just couldn't stand the clothes. Department threads—dead.

The call from the private investigator had disrupted his plan to knock off a bit early so that he could spend a few more minutes with Molly. Hey, it had worked out. He had cruised by the station on the way to the detective's office, changed from his uniform to slacks, collarless shirt, and loafers, and signed out with a notation that he had one more visit to make before the official end of his shift. Hear what the detective wanted, spend as little time as possible with the guy, then hop over to Molly's. Never know what might transpire. She had been more and more friendly with each visit. Maybe tonight was the night.

Eugene Nieto normally wouldn't have bothered with a prompt response to a call from a private dick. They weren't worth his time. Glorified process servers. Wanna-bes. Security guards. Hotel detectives, if there was still such a thing. Not the kind of people for whom Eugene would go out of his way. He could have made Mora come to him, strung him along by insisting on an appointment at the station, then canceled at the last minute, rescheduled. Maybe, finally, one day gotten together with the guy.

But this wasn't the usual case. Not the time for the normal routine. Mora had said he needed to talk about the Kiko Vigil murder, that Vigil thing again. Play it cozy, meet the guy, find out what the hell he's doing puttering around that case. The Vigil thing made Nieto nervous, and when he was nervous, he took extra steps to be careful. Accommodating Mora by meeting with him at his office was the least Nieto could do, and the safest, considering.

The Vigil thing had been sloppy, he knew that, and so did others. He had answered more questions from other cops and Internal Affairs geeks than he should have had to, but it was impossible to avoid the scrutiny that the shooting of Kiko Vigil had generated. His reports had been incomplete, sometimes useless, and his overall handling of the crime scene that night, waiting for the homicide crew, had been severely criticized. He had been disciplined in clever ways that the department had to teach new cops hard lessons. A short suspension, standard. But then they added traffic control, in the snow. Rousting homeless bums along the Cherry

Creek bike path at midnight. Cleaning up horseshit for the horse patrol crew. Acting the fool, and running like one from the dogs training for the canine patrol, just to keep his ass in one piece.

But all that was over, in the past. He had skated away from that, and now he was ready, a new outlook, new responsibilities. Maybe he had a future in law enforcement after all.

Except that this guy Mora, probably a dropout from the academy, was dragging the carcass of that dead case to the sunlight. For what? What could he possibly have to do with Kiko Vigil?

By the time he arrived at Mora's, he had worked himself into an acute case of anxiety. Sweat had stained his fresh clothes.

Nieto didn't like Danny Mora's office. Too dark, with strange faces on the wall. Enough to give a guy the creeps. And Mora. He definitely was something else.

"So, Mr. Mora, what can I do for you? About this Kiko Vigil matter. Your call didn't really explain much. If you have some new information about that shooting, I'll be happy to take it. Have to admit, though, that the case is pretty cold. That was a tough one. Not a lot of good leads."

His voice trailed off because of Mora's unremitting stare. It was a strange stare, without detail; a man looking straight at him, straight into him. Nieto wished there was more light in the office so he could get a good look at the other man, so he could tell what was going on in the guy's head. If he could just look in his eyes, watch him as he talked.

The dark face finally spoke.

"I've been hired to go over the case, in an unofficial way. A friend of the victim wants me to wrap up what I can. I've been looking over reports, talking to a few witnesses. Your name came up often. The first cop at the scene, the officer who tried to organize the layout. Must have been crazy, that night. What with the shooting and the crowd at the bar?"

Nieto worked very hard on what he thought was a careful answer.

"A friend of the victim? That's hinky, man. But I guess you take clients wherever you can get them, eh?"

Mora didn't respond.

Nieto realized he had to give the investigator something or the meeting might never end.

"Anyway, that's the way those scenes always are. I've handled plenty like that. My beat for a long time has been over there on Larimer, up into Curtis Park. Got everything from hard-core dealers to wetbacks to drunk college kids. All of the guys on duty that night, we did what we could. But like you say, it was crazy out there."

Mora's steady, deep voice said, "Officer, let me tell you a few things that I'm thinking. You then can tell me if I'm way off base, if I'm close, or, maybe, that I got it right on the head. What do you say?"

Nieto twisted in his seat. "Whatever. This is your show." He waited for Mora.

"One thing I found, looking things over, was about this potential witness in a wheelchair. Frankie Johns. Remember him?"

Nieto almost laughed out loud. The crip in the chair? That's what this was all about?

"I got something in my report about that guy. I remember something about him. He was hanging around that night. That's the kind of weirdo he was. Gawker. Didn't help out much, as I recall." He paused, took a breath. "Why?"

"There's a chance," Mora answered, "that he saw more than you got out of him. Might have seen the shooter. You get any indication of that, maybe something that didn't go in your report?"

"Hey, you know that can't happen," Nieto sputtered. "I put everything down in those reports that I saw, or heard, or was told. Goddamn paperwork enough to drive me crazy. But I do it. That's one thing you got to stay on top of in the department—the paperwork. So, if there was anything about the wheelchair guy seeing somebody, I would have noted it. Since apparently I didn't, then it wasn't anything I found out. See how that works?"

Mora worked kinks out of his neck by rotating his head. His hunch about Nieto was correct. The guy was too defensive, too self-righteous to just be a lazy cop. There was more to it.

He asked, "Know where he is? Anything about him? I'd like to talk with him, if it's possible. What do you say?"

Clean Gene Nieto thought, I was right. A big damn waste of time.

He said, with exaggerated patience, "I told you. If I knew anything, it goes down in my report. If, like you say, you read my reports, then that's it. There ain't nothing else. Anyway, I heard later, after the case had been put to sleep as far as I was concerned, I heard that the crip left town. Texas, I think it was, San Antonio. Frankie Johns was a hustler, a bum. If that's what's got you all fired up, it ain't much."

"I disagree," Mora said, still easy. "Johns was, is, a solid lead. Someone that you did your best to keep away from others who worked the case. Why is that, Officer? Why did you do such a crummy job of asking this man questions? At the scene of a very violent shooting of a fellow law enforcement officer? If anything, you should have been more aggressive with this witness just because of the victim, yet, it was almost like you could hardly take any time to do your job. I got to ask again. Why?"

Nieto's frustration got the better of him. "What is this? What kind of game you trying to play? Do you have information on this case or not? I'm warning you, if you're withholding information, expecting some kind of reward or something, then you're in for more trouble than it's worth. Withholding information on a homicide will not only get you a lot more attention from the homicide guys than you ever want, it could probably mean the end of your career as an investigator. Not good for business, you see what I mean?"

Mora's tone stayed level, but Nieto felt the threat in the words.

"Stop it, Nieto. I've read through more pages on Kiko Vigil than you can even imagine. I've talked to far better cops than you about Kiko Vigil. I've done more on this case than you ever thought about."

Nieto tried to stare down the other man, but it was impossible with the way the lighting worked in the office. He wasn't ready for the barrage of abuse that Mora threw at him.

"You're a disgrace to the badge. Your work was bad, very bad. I know about your suspension. I know about the official inquiry about your handling of the initial crime scene. And I know that you have to accept a lot of the blame for the fact that no one has ever been brought down for killing Kiko Vigil. Who, by the way, was a good cop."

"What the fuck! Are you crazy? You know who you're talking to? I could have you dragged downtown. You got a lot of nerve, asshole, trying to bust my balls about Kiko Vigil. Who the hell are you?"

Mora knew he had the upper hand.

"I'm the guy you didn't want to meet. Not about this case, not about any case. I've taken a real personal interest in the murder of Kiko Vigil. You know why, Nieto? A friend of mine, a real good friend, died recently. And the way I look at it, he died because of what happened around Vigil. Probably the same killer. Some connection that I don't understand yet, but it's there. And another thing you got to know. I feel really bad because it looks like some of this is my fault. At least what happened to my friend. That's what I wanted to tell you, Officer. I know you fucked up. I'm looking close at what's gone down, and I ain't going away. I just wanted you to know. Wanted you to think about that. And if there's anything you want to tell me, now is the time. You may not get another chance."

Nieto couldn't believe what he had just heard. He wanted to leap across the desk, pound the man, take out his weapon and use it on the man's head, lock him up for a few nights. He convinced himself to stay in check.

"You are one crazy motherfucker, Mora. I'm going to get the hell out of here before I do something that you won't like. Crazy. Crazy."

He ran out of the office and quickly got in his car. He had lost all thought about Molly. He turned on his cell phone, dialed the number he had memorized many months before. The sweat was rolling in huge drops down his ribs and along the waistband of his designer boxer shorts.

"It's me. Gene. Yeah. Fuck you, man! We got trouble. This guy, this fucking detective. He just gave me a raft of shit about Vigil. He knows something, man. I'm telling you. Yeah, yeah. Sure. You'll take care of it. That's what you been saying, Fidel, but it ain't taken care of yet. Clean this up. I've had enough grief. You ain't paid me enough for this. Now, you do what you have to."

From his window, Danny Mora could see a car parked in the street, and in the car, the shadow of Eugene Nieto speaking frantically into a phone. On a pad he kept in the top drawer of his desk Danny Mora made a note of his conversation with the policeman and then wrote two additional words.

San Antonio?

■

"David. We got to get out of here. This heat. Lousy tourists ain't good for nothing. Cheap bastards. Hate to say it, but we got to leave. We tried, gave it a shot, a real shot. We got pushed out of the Alamo and throwed out of the airport. Denver sounds good now. At least I had a place. At least we could get a job every once in a while. We're going back, David. Back to Denver. You can get your old job back; maybe I can find a gig with my ax. Texas is not our place. We don't belong here. Hate to say it, but we got to leave. Understand? Hope we didn't burn any bridges."

David the Dancer squinted at Billy Cordero, who called himself Frankie. He didn't understand. What did bridges have to do with Denver? They had slept under a bridge in San Antonio, but as far as he could remember, they hadn't burned anything, except old rags for a little light that one time, but that couldn't be what Billy meant, of course. It was sometimes pretty damn hard to figure out just what the hell Billy was talking about, but he did mention Denver, and Denver had been good—at least there had been the flower job and the dance, he could get back to the dance.

"David, you listening? You're gone again, damn. Try to pay attention, David. We got to get our stuff together, scrape together as much money as we can. Head out on that highway. Back to Denver. We got friends there, David. Not like these bossy Texans. We got some real friends in Colorado. More I think about it, the more I like the idea. Back to Denver. Back home."

■

Danny Mora and Robert Spann sat across from each other in a booth in the Bella Vista, a restaurant on the edge of downtown and within walking distance of Spann's office. The place was packed with the usual lunchtime crowd from the businesses in the area. Lawyers, their secretaries, bank cashiers, salesmen from a burglar alarm company, and navy recruiters feasted on the Mexican cuisine that had captured the attention of a steady and loyal daytime following. The delay between sitting down and ordering was legendary, but the food more than compensated.

Spann and Mora didn't look out of place. The tall, lean white man wearing a tie and a nondescript sports coat could have been trying to sell the dark, tough-looking Chicano the latest security system. They could have been reviewing computerized alarms, access codes, video cameras, and motion lights. The constant hum from the other customers and the intermittent kitchen noise made conversations safe, private, and the two men talked about murder at a leisurely pace and in a regular tone.

Spann asked, "Even if the same guy killed Delgado and Chávez, why do you think he's got a connection to Garza? That's a lot of blood for file folders and cassette tapes."

"You told me Garza was very methodic, almost obsessive," Mora explained. "He demanded the tapes and files. Delgado held out for a payoff, then Garza decided to quit wasting time and put his man on the job. That man kills Delgado and Chávez as part of his job. I think he's the same shooter that hit Vigil. There's a common link between the three, and that's Garza, if we accept that the killer was looking for something in Delgado's office and my house. That could only be the stuff I took from Delgado. It's enough of a connection for me. We find the killer of my friend, and we solve the killing of your friend, too."

Spann nodded impassively.

"Looks like you're out of a job. This guy is a madman, and he knows you have what he wants. I'm sorry I got you involved. You need to pull back. If you turn over the information to the cops, it gets out that you don't have what Garza wants. You walk away from all this."

"Too late for that," Mora disagreed. "I have to assume this guy can think things through like me. He knows I can make the link between Delgado, Tomás, Vigil, and Garza. If there was anything that I wasn't supposed to learn, that's already happened. Anyway, I want him as much as he wants me. More."

Mora's words bothered Spann, but he couldn't do much about that. He no longer believed that Mora was working for him, that Mora was only the hired investigator looking into the death of Kiko Vigil. Tomás Chávez had changed that.

Spann said, "There's something else. The hit man may be too busy for you just now. The Garza people are otherwise occupied; know what I mean? Denver is hot for them. Those tapes, and you, may not be their first priority."

"What's going on?"

Spann's eyes swept the restaurant crowd. He had to be careful.

"The Cardoza-Garza businesses are in trouble. There's a vacuum of leadership in Garza's outfit. No one's stepped up to replace Lorraine, and Garza won't leave Mexico. So, naturally, there's new competition. They've taken over some of the more lucrative interests."

Mora said, "Wonder what the hell happened to her? Nothing on her since Vigil died?"

Spann shook his head. "Nada. She's probably dead, too. Not many people survive double crossing Elías Garza."

"So, in a way, Vigil succeeded," Mora added.

The men continued eating. When he looked up from his food, Spann said, "There's more. I hope I can trust you, man." He didn't expect the detective to reassure him. "Someone's carrying out a personal wrecking job on what remains in the hands of Cardoza/Garza. Our office has been tipped off in the last few days to three major shipments of illegals. We rounded them up and shipped them back. What's important, though, is we got our hands on some of the major coyotes. Guys we've been chasing for years. They were out in the open, red-handed, and we knew exactly where to find them. Our agency isn't the only one. Denver PD, FBI, DEA, ATF—all have made major busts or raids on the basis of information from the inside. There's a lot of illegal dope piling up in federal warehouses."

"Any idea who? Or why? The informant might be helpful in tracking Tomás's killer."

"No clue as to who," Spann said. "The why is what I call criminal evolution. Hoodlums tend to turn on each other. Nature of the beast. Sooner or later, it happens. Of course, usually not in such a big way as this. Drugs, guns, bags of money, even a planeload of teenage girls from Mexico City for prostitution, complete with a pair of bastards who thought they were going to be big-time pimps in *los estados unidos*."

"I haven't heard anything about this. Nothing in the papers, on the news. Why no coverage?"

"Politics, Danny. What else? This shit has been under the surface of squeaky-clean Denver. This city's almost too good to be true. The mayor, governor, certain businessmen. They've leaned on all of us to downplay what's happened— what's happening. The reality of all this crime might scare away the tourists, the baseball fans, the conventions lined up for next summer. Not to mention the drunk kids in Lodo on Friday nights, just a few blocks from where Kiko had his last date with Lorraine Garza. There's been a crime wave, but it's been a quiet one. The roundup will be even quieter."

Danny Mora pushed away a plate that had held green chile, beans, and rice. He said, "Like I told you the first time we met—I don't get worked up about illegal immigration. Not my idea of a crime wave."

Spann let a smile curve his mouth.

"I could almost agree with you. But that ain't official, okay? My job depends on illegal immigration, crime wave or not. Besides, Cardoza and Garza are in more heavy stuff than just illegals. Their cargo is human, dope, guns, so on. Some of it *is* scary. Keeps me off the streets at night."

Now it was Mora's turn to smile.

"Okay, Spann. There's a major crisis going on with the Cardoza-Garza enterprises. Arrests, raids. Maybe our boy, the killer, has outlived his usefulness. Seems to me we got to get to him if you want to have any chance of finding the truth about Kiko Vigil. But realistically, we may have to just wait for him to make the next move."

Spann accepted Mora's conclusion. "Yeah, that sounds right." He finished the last piece of a tortilla. His *chile rellenos* were gone. "I brought the pictures you asked for. What gives? Why old photos of Garza?"

Mora said, "The ones I've seen are bad. Nothing real clear. Even the surveillance shots from the FBI are of Garza in a big hat, or under an umbrella, or surrounded by others. What I've seen, I'm not sure I would recognize him if he waited on us here at this restaurant. So, I want to see others just in case, that's all. I try to minimize the chances for surprises."

"Garza is a very careful man," Spann said.

He pushed a manila envelope across the table.

"They're yours, Danny. Nothing real old. The guy didn't exist, officially, until about ten years ago, and by then he was in the inner sanctum of the Cardoza organization. There's a shot in here of him back then, shoulder to shoulder with the PRI candidate for governor of the state of Jalisco. We got a copy that night, just in time, it seems. The photographer, a freelancer trying to make a peso selling photos to the Mexican tabloids, had an accident a few days later. Word was he was very drunk, drove his car off the cliffs at Acapulco. All of his stuff—cameras, negatives, prints—went down in the crash. Ironic, no?"

Mora nodded. He thought Robert Spann had a strange way of looking at things.

"**W**e have to take it easy, Lorraine. Santiago is ready to kill somebody, anybody. He knows you're the one that's been tipping off the cops. He wants me to bring you in. All the heat on the operations, it's made Elías as angry as he's ever been. You know how he gets when he's angry."

Lorraine touched the thin scar along her jawline. She knew all about Elías Garza's anger.

She turned her back on Fidel. She spoke to the wall, listening for his reaction.

"We've only started. I thought you were with me on this. I don't only want to hurt Elías. I'm going to bring him down! You can go along for the ride, Fidel. Or you can sit back and watch. It's up to you. Santiago doesn't scare me. He's another one of Elías's toadies. *Hace la pelotilla.* You take care of him, I'll do the rest."

The man rubbed his eyes, rubbed his hair, tried to think as clearly as he could. He grabbed her shoulders.

She's right, of course. Aim at Garza's hold on the operation. Why else gamble everything I've built up, everything I have? Now Santiago's on my ass, breathing fire. And that's not all. That private detective, Mora. Getting too close. Have to do something about him, too. He'll be easy. Supposed to be a tough guy. Challenge his machismo and he'll come running to me like a greyhound in heat.

He mumbled in her ear. "*Querida,* don't be like that. I thought we had something, I thought it was us two, together? You've changed, Lorraine. There was that first couple of nights, remember? But lately, it's like all you got on your mind is Elías, and the business."

Lorraine wanted to cringe. Instead she turned and held him close.

The man is such an idiot! He actually believes there could be something between us. He killed Kiko, he does Elías's bidding like a lapdog. He's a dead man. I will have to kill him, when it's time, when he is no longer useful. And if I don't, if I fail, Elías will take care of him. Please, Blessed Virgin, let his soul burn in hell forever. Pig! Cabrón!

She wanted to sound strong and steady. "We have too much to do. Later, after, there will be time for us, you and me. We have to be careful. Keep our wits."

"I don't know." He panted in her face. "Santiago is talking heavy, making noises about doing something. Elías is leaning on him bad. He's afraid."

"Does he suspect you? Haven't you convinced him that you are doing everything you can to plug the leak?"

The man let her go. Now he turned away.

"He may kill me just to have something to report to Elías. It doesn't matter to him. Elías does that to people. That's how he's been the boss for so long. Fear, lady. He controls with fear."

Behind his back she shook her head.

He's losing his nerve. He's going to run or turn me in to Santiago.

She said, "We can take care of Santiago. Why not? We nail him, like the others. Set him up, let the cops have him."

"Ha!" He made a fist and shook it at the ceiling. "Santiago ain't that stupid. He's not going to put himself in jeopardy. Not with the way things are falling apart. I haven't even seen the guy for days. Everything is by pay phone. Nah, it would have to be something very special, almost priceless to get him to come out of wherever it is he's holed up."

She grabbed him again and looked directly in the face of the man she hated as much as she hated Elías Garza. Her lips parted slightly, and her voice came out husky and sweet.

"Okay, Fidel. Maybe you're right. Maybe we do need some relaxation. Come here. Help me. Make yourself comfortable. Let's see what we can do to take your mind off big, bad Santiago."

Fidel smiled broadly. He undid his belt, then helped Lorraine with the buttons on her skirt. They kissed.

Finally she understood. *Fidel, Santiago, Elías, Kiko. Does any of it matter? It has to stop. I'm ready. Whatever happens, I am ready.*

"But baby, it is time for us to take care of Santiago. Tell him you found me. Set it up that you know where I'll be, tomorrow night. I'll be alone. He can take care of me all by himself, get back in Elías's favor. He wants the Juárez job, this is the way to win it. That should jerk him out of his rat nest. That's why he's here, to get me. Make it sound easy. I'm too strung out over Kiko, over wanting to hurt Elías, to think clearly. I'll be alone, at one of the warehouses, looking for more ways to hurt the operation. There won't be anyone there except me. Then I'll do what I have to do. Okay, baby, okay?"

He heard her talking, but he wasn't really listening.

Her plan is wild, stupid. Santiago will kill her. But . . . if she pulls it off, good for her. Lorraine is the one woman who might be able to do it. Either way, I have nothing to lose. They can slaughter each other for all I care. Whoever walks away, Fidel will be okay. On top, as usual.

He had played it perfectly. He deserved it. He had been loyal, patient. All the ugly work Elías had needed, that he had ordered. Dumped on him like a flunky. Years of responding like a trained dog. In two days, it would all be his. With Santiago's story of how Fidel had helped, Garza would give it to him; there was no one else. If Lorraine survived, then he would run it with her, for a while, until he removed her, too. He had to take care of one more detail. The detective. One more small point. And that would be it.

He was about to collect all he was owed, all he had ever wanted.

Now, right now, he wanted something else from her, and he was going to get it.

■

He slept on the couch in the small waiting room. He kept a

razor in the rest room. His life centered on what he could accomplish in his office, or, if necessary, outside, in the city, as long as it had to do with Tomás, or Delgado, or Kiko Vigil.

He answered the first call around nine-thirty, in darkness. He had been sitting at his desk, without light. His thoughts were crazy with images of Tomás, Delgado's photos of Silvia Compeán, news clippings about Garza, and, in the background, the voice of Patricia Montelibre. The ringing of the phone yanked him from his daze, and he was disoriented when he said hello to Robert Spann.

"I thought you'd be there instead of your house." Spann's voice was hoarse, or cloaked. "I may get tossed out of the agency for this. But I think you should know. The FBI got another tip about one of Garza's operations. They let us in on it because of possible illegal alien action, too. Tomorrow night, after midnight, there's a guy every federal law enforcement agency would give up half of its next year's budget for. Santiago Jiménez, one of the major lieutenants in the Cardoza-Garza mob. He's going to be at the Geeso Brothers warehouse down along the South Platte, on Jason. An import-export outfit, perfect cover. He could be our guy, Danny. If he's not the shooter, then he sure as hell knows who is. This is a break for us. I'll let you know if we get anything out of the guy. I'll call you day after tomorrow."

The second call came at eleven.

"Danny Mora?"

"Yeah. Who's this?"

"Uh, ah, it's just that, uh, like, we just got back and right away everybody's telling us that you been asking around about us, saying that you wanted to talk with us. Even offered money, they said. And, uh, so, ah, we got your number out of the book and so, uh, ah, I'm calling to see what this is all about?"

One thousand one. One thousand two. Mora made the connection.

"Frankie Johns? Is this Frankie Johns?" Mora hollered at the phone.

"Well, yeah. Real name's Billy, Billy Cordero, but I calls myself Frankie, from way back, before I ever got to Denver, before I—"

Mora interrupted, "Yeah, okay, Frankie, Billy, whatever. I have been looking for you. Where the hell you been? I heard you were in Texas."

Billy waited, then realized he should say something. "Oh, we been around. South? You know how it is. So, uh, ah, what's this all about?"

"I need to talk with you, Frankie. You are a very important man. A witness to something that happened months ago. You may know something that could help out in a very important investigation. When can I talk with you?"

Billy's mind clouded with too many implications from the detective's words. "Witness? I don't think so. I ain't witnessed nothing in a long time, not since Nam, not since before that, really."

"No, Frankie, you don't understand. You might have seen something that even you don't know how important it could be. Look, we just should talk in person. I'll come to you. When? Where?"

"Hey, you want to talk with me, fine. Is there, like, a reward or something? Some money or something like that. Is that right?"

"Yes, Frankie. A thousand dollars if you got information

like I think you got. Information that leads to a man I'm looking for. I'll give you a hundred just for your trouble, no matter if you don't know anything. What do you say? When? Where?"

Billy perked up. "Whoa! A thousand bucks. You sure you're looking for me?"

"Positive, my man. You and nobody else."

"Well, hey, I'll talk to you. Sure, why not? Could use a hundred anytime. But mister, what's this about? What do you think I witnessed?"

"Earlier in the year. In front of the Tortuga Bar. There was a shooting. You were there. At least, that's what you told a cop that night. Right? Remember that?"

Billy had half expected that the shooting would come back to him, and here it was.

"Oh, shit. Yeah. I remember that. Fucker nearly ruined my chair. Ran right into me. He didn't help me, either. Just carried out that lady and dumped her in the car. Then another guy plowed over me. Happened a lot that night. That's what you want to see me about? Shoot, man. If that's what it is, then you get my grand ready. I'm your man, mister."

The third call happened at one-thirty in the morning. He had curled up in his chair, not asleep but not fully awake, papers from the Elías Garza file scattered around his desk and at his feet. His shirt stuck to his warm skin.

Her voice sounded cool, fresh.

"Danny? What are you still doing there? You need rest. Go home, get some sleep."

"What are you doing calling me at this time? How do you know I wasn't sleeping?"

"I know."

"Couldn't sleep, either, could you? You're the one who needs rest. This thing will wear you out. Take a trip, get out of town, go to . . ."

"Stop it. That's not going to happen. For either one of us. We both aren't letting this go. We're in it together, whether we want to be or not. I'm coming over. You can tell me what you've learned, what happens next."

He didn't argue with her. The hot, long night had opened a weak spot at his core. Nothing seemed as clear to him as everything once had.

He said, "There is one thing. A tip about a man who may be the one we all want. I'm going to find him tomorrow. Tomorrow night. This may all be over then, tomorrow night. Could be finished, if that's the way it falls out. Tomorrow night."

"You don't sound good. I'm on my way."

The darkness and the silence and the heat returned. The masks watched his back, and he took comfort from knowing that they were there. He waited for Patricia Montelibre.

■

She found him sitting in the dark, bleary-eyed, depressed. She wanted to grab his hands and rub them, to make the blood flow back in his heart. She pulled the chain on his desk lamp and offered him a glass of water.

She whispered, "Danny. You need to take care of yourself. Why are you doing this? What sense is there working yourself to exhaustion?"

He tried to sound alert. "Don't worry about me. I'm just

working extra hours, that's all. I get this way, when I'm close to finishing a tough case. I'll be all right."

"I doubt it. Here, let me get you some more water."

In the office rest room she half filled the glass with cold water. She took a drink herself, then carried the glass back to Danny.

"I have to worry about you. Don't you know that? You're all that remains of Tomás. You and he were more than friends; you were brothers, at least. There's a lot of Tomás in you, just like there was a lot of you in him."

She handed Danny the half-empty glass of water, but before he grabbed it, she lost her grip. The glass crashed on the carpet, broke into several pieces, and water quickly soaked the rug. She jumped back, agitated, frightened. A high-pitched whimper escaped her throat. Her lips trembled. He heard her sobs.

He said, "Hey, it's all right. It's just water. No harm. Let me clean up the glass."

He realized she wasn't upset about the broken glass. Large tears flowed down her face although she clenched her eyes, tried to not let him see her cry.

He brought her into his arms.

She cried against his warm chest, and he could feel her own warmth and the fury that she held since Tomás's death. He didn't know what to say. Her arms wrapped around him and drew him even closer.

Her moist eyes reflected the glare from the desk lamp.

Their mouths found each other. They fell to the wet carpet. They rolled on the carpet, kissing, oblivious to the pieces of broken glass, holding each other as though a gale tore at them, threatening to rip them apart.

Mora gently pushed away. He let go of her. He said what they both knew.

"This isn't what we need."

She agreed with her silence.

She rubbed her hands across her face.

"I'm sorry. Sorry I cried again, sorry for . . ."

"Don't. It will be all right."

■

She drifted off to sleep in the makeshift bed that Danny had used the several nights he hadn't left the office. A couple of old blankets he had taken from his house, cushions from the couch, and the hard support of the floor of his office would have to do. Patricia hadn't objected. He remained awake. Fragmented thoughts about Tomás mingled with the rusty taste of betrayal.

The shrill and abrasive ringing of the telephone signaled the fourth call that night. It shook him and startled Patricia. She sat up, pulling the blankets around her.

"This is Mora. Who's this?"

A voice with a faint accent said, "Hope I didn't wake you, man. That cute little Patricia been keeping you up? She could do it, huh? Really nice tits on that one. I got something for her, too, if she tags along. Tell her it will be a lot more fun than what's going to happen to you. If you got the nerve, that is."

"Who is this? What the fuck do you want?"

"I'm the man you've been looking for, Mora. You know, the guy who sliced open your friend. What was that guy's name? Chávez, wasn't it? You should have been there, Mora. Your friend cried like a baby. Cried for you, in fact.

Guess he didn't think it was fair that he ended up dead because of you."

"You sonofabitch!"

Patricia jumped to her feet and ran to his side. Danny held the receiver away from his ear, and they both could hear the man on the other end.

"Easy, man. Don't get all riled up, not yet. You've been poking around about Kiko Vigil and your dead buddy. You got something to ask, why not come to me? The horse's mouth. What you say, Mora? Up for a chance to end this thing, once and for all? Got the balls to meet me, face-to-face? I still got that blade I used on your friend. It will work just fine on you."

Mora was eager. "Sure, tell me where you are. Then I get on the phone to the cops. Are you really that stupid?"

"Good, Mora. Shows you're thinking, although it's damn late. No, man. You ain't going to the cops. I got something you want. I got the goods on Garza, on Kiko Vigil, and a few others you don't even know about. And of course, there's always me. Maybe you owe your pal something? It's all yours, if you can get to me, that is. So, Danny Mora. It's your move."

He gave Danny an address and told him that he would be there at four-thirty that morning. Then he hung up.

There had been no way to keep Patricia from coming along, but he managed to convince her to wait in the car and to call the police on her cell phone if anything went wrong. It already felt wrong, so he wasn't sure what she was supposed to wait for, but that was where they had left it.

She reluctantly agreed only after she convinced herself that she couldn't talk him out of the meeting.

He had her park the car a block away from the house. A small .25-caliber Beretta rested in his shoulder holster. He left Patricia sitting in the car with the phone and another gun.

The Victorian house sat back from the street, its north side covered with brown ivy and impotent rose vines. A busted streetlight hovered uselessly around tired shade trees. Weeds, patches of dead lawn, and gray dirt filled the yard behind a gray, rickety picket fence.

A weather-beaten for-sale sign stood crookedly near a clump of spindly thistle. Under the weak light of a far-off blinking neon sign, the thistle blooms appeared black against the night sky.

He walked around the house, using a cracked walk that curved next to the vanished lawn, and slowly worked his way to the back. He paused every few feet, listening for anything. The farther he ventured, the more difficulty he had making out any details. The backyard was almost completely black. The insignificant amount of illumination from the front didn't pierce this side of the house. He peered in a grimy, streaked window at what looked like an empty living room. Nothing. He took the Beretta from his holster and held it in his right hand.

I'll have to get in. Why would he pick this place? Does he live around here? Maybe next door, watching my every move? Inside waiting for me? Got the door booby-trapped? It's almost four-thirty. Where is he?

The sound in the alley was nothing more than a scrape, a misstep of a soft-soled shoe on summer-warm asphalt. Danny Mora threw himself away from the house and landed with a thud on the ground. He squinted. Nothing but darkness.

For a few minutes he lay where he had landed, scanning shadows against the general charcoal of the night. Trees, a fence, a bush of some sort. He raised his head an inch.

He felt, rather than heard, the swoosh, and instinctively he rolled to his side. A rush of air next to his head buzzed his ear. Someone had tried to kick his head. He kept rolling.

Something landed on him and knocked the air out of his lungs. A pair of hands gripped his throat. He couldn't bring in new air to his body. The hands tightened even as he tried to shake off the weight that pinned him on the ground.

The man grunted. Mora couldn't see his face.

Danny Mora tried to lift his legs, but they were held in a vise of muscle and bone that he couldn't move. His arms were pinned at his sides, held by the same vise. He shook his head, gagging for air. Dizzy, light-headed, he knew he was passing out.

The man's iron-tight grip closed around his throat. Danny Mora couldn't breathe.

"Danny! Danny!"

Patricia's screams echoed in his numb brain, the words bouncing with the pops and crackles of his strangulation. The weight that had held him down suddenly lifted. Air rushed into his lungs, and he gulped for more.

He saw Patricia on the back of the man, hitting him with the butt of her gun.

Danny tried to put together a picture that could help him. The shadow in front of him violently twisted and jumped. Patricia's voice screamed again.

"Help! Police! Help!"

The man shook off Patricia, and the shadow split in two. She crawled to Danny and forced him to his feet. She dragged him to the back door. The man pulled a gun from his waist and without thinking, without aiming, jerked the trigger. The shot screamed through the windowpane. For the second time that night, glass crashed around them. Patricia screamed and fell on the concrete steps below the door.

She reached up and seized the doorknob. She turned it and nothing happened.

Danny saw Patricia's hand on the doorknob and covered it with his. They pushed on the door together. They heard movements like a panting dog dragging itself across the dirt.

Danny shoved his shoulder against the door. It gave an inch.

The man pulled the trigger again and, behind them, the night erupted. Patricia and Danny tumbled into the house, through the broken door. They landed on the dusty floor and rolled away from the doorway.

A police siren wailed in the street. The man ran from the yard and down the alley.

Danny got to his knees. His chest throbbed, burned, and he tasted blood. He forced several large gulps of air down his throat.

Then he heard the groans.

"Ohhh."

"Patricia!" His voice cracked. He managed to ask, "Are you all right?"

She had tumbled into a corner.

He placed his arms under her and lifted her head. She could only moan. Blood flowed onto the old wooden floor of the house and mixed with dust and cobwebs.

■

"Something happen to your throat, huh? Must be tough to not be able to talk as much as you want. Would be for me. But then, people say I talk too much anyway, sometimes. Other times, I'm quiet like a mouse, don't even know I'm around. Except when I play my ax. Then you know I'm around. So's what's the deal, man?"

While he talked, Billy Cordero stared at the man's weird masks on the walls, but even he knew that they were unusual decor for an office. Unless private eyes were like that. Unusual, that is.

Danny had to whisper his words. The doctor had told him not to talk unless it was absolutely necessary. He needed to prevent further damage to his vocal cords and larynx, and, in the doctor's opinion, not talking appeared the best way to do that.

For Danny, talking with Frankie Johns was absolutely necessary. He might have seen the face of the man who had tried to crush his trachea, the man who had killed Tomás.

"Like I said, I can't talk much. I would like for you to look at these pictures and tell me if you see anyone you know."

The words burned his throat.

Billy decided he was happy he had called the detective. It had turned into an adventure.

"You mean the guy who ran me over at the Tortuga, right?" he said excitedly. "Think he's in these pictures, huh? You think he did the shooting, don't you? I know he took that woman out of there. Her all covered with blood. Don't mind telling you, I was kind of glad he didn't pay more attention to me."

Billy fanned photographs that included those that Robert Spann had passed on to Danny and others that the detective had collected from newspapers and the files of Kiko Vigil and Victor Delgado.

He looked at each one for several minutes, eyeing them closely, inspecting them. Occasionally he would comment about an attractive woman or a man's colorful tie.

Finally he said, "Hey, look at this, would you?"

Mora's back straightened. "Somebody you recognize?"

"Sure. Of course. Right here. This picture at this ballpark. That's Fernando Valenzuela in the middle of all these guys in the suits. Doesn't look too comfortable, does he?"

Danny Mora didn't know what Frankie Johns was talking about, but he let him go through the pictures at his own pace, in his own way.

Danny couldn't identify the man who had jumped him on Curtis Street. It had all happened in the black yard of the empty house, too quickly, and he hadn't been able to help the police with any kind of description except that he was a strong man with powerful hands. Patricia also hadn't provided any help. She had lunged at the man's back, then struggled with him while she tried to hit him with the gun. She should have shot him when she had the chance, she had groused from her bed in the emergency ward, but she hadn't fired because she feared hitting the wrong man.

Billy Cordero jumped about six inches and squealed, "Hey! That's him. Son of a gun. There's the guy. Right there."

Danny grabbed the photo that Billy had been fingering.

"Here. This guy? That's Elías Garza. It can't be. No way."

"Sure is, mister. The man that dumped me out of my chair is that same guy, right there. Right there."

He pointed at a man in the picture. Danny expected the bony finger to rest on Garza, who was half hidden by an umbrella as he walked along a rainy Mexico City street. But Billy Cordero, who called himself Frankie, aimed for and hit another man, walking away from Garza, in the opposite direction. A man who didn't look like he even was with Garza, a passerby on the street who wouldn't be noticed.

Billy sweated. He worked hard to make his point. There was too much money at stake for the detective not to believe him.

"That's the guy—I'd bet on it. I'd bet that thousand bucks you're going to give me. Let me know if you find him, mister. I'll tell anybody who wants to know. That's the guy who ran out of the Tortuga, carrying a woman over his shoulder, and the same guy who knocked me over. I would of told that cop that night, if he would of listened. That's the way it is, and sometimes you can't do anything about the way things are. I know that's been the way it is with me, more times than not. Life. Can't live with it, can't live without it. Say, where's that thousand?"

■

Although three different law enforcement agencies were involved, the task force members dressed in the same outfit: flak jackets, black helmets, dark blue fatigues. They had been on-site for more than an hour and, before them, a trio of men had watched the building since dawn until the task force had arrived. All were convinced that no one remained in the building and that no other people were in the area. No drivers, lookouts, or additional security.

A man entered the building shortly after midnight, just as the law officers had been warned. Fifteen minutes later, a second car stopped in the otherwise deserted parking lot and a woman dressed in a suede jacket with fringe hurried into the building.

Robert Spann sucked in his breath, then shook his

head. He wasn't too old for surprises. Lorraine Garza. She was the leak, the informant wrecking her husband's criminal empire.

The FBI man in charge barked an order through his helmet's transmitter. "All units, position one. Wait for the signal for position two."

Spann and his group of four agents inched their way across the parking lot and hunched under the rim of a metal window ledge. They waited for the command to crash through the side door that had been designated as theirs. A dozen similar groups of men and women crawled to their prearranged places around the building.

Spann heard the words "yellow light" through his earpiece. He patted the man next to him on the shoulder, and this was repeated with each of the four men Spann had in his command.

Two of the men planted a rectangular metal box at the foot of the door. The group backed ten feet away from the door, then they sprawled on the asphalt of the parking lot.

"Green! Go! Go!"

An explosion rocked the far side of the building, and Spann felt the ground roll beneath him. An orange flash lit up the inside of the building. Spann tripped a switch on a control unit that hung from his belt. The box leaning on the metal door exploded and, amid smoke and another incandescent flash, the door blew inward. Spann and his men rushed the warehouse.

Santiago Jiménez crouched on the concrete floor, frantically waving a massive handgun. He gripped the right arm of Lorraine Garza, who twisted on her knees in front of Jiménez. Spann split away from his men while they knelt in a circle, their automatic rifles aimed in different directions. Other task force members entered the building from all sides, through doors and shattered windows. Jiménez futilely kicked at a smoke grenade near his feet.

In the billowing green fog, the man in charge shouted at Jiménez.

"Federal Bureau of Investigation! Drop your weapon and turn the woman loose! You have five seconds or you're a dead man!"

Jiménez's eyes were wild, crazy, frozen with fear and hatred. He squeezed Lorraine's arm.

The women squirmed in his grasp. She said, "It's over, Santiago. Over for you and Elías. You finally pay for what you did to Kiko."

Jiménez shouted, "Shut up, bitch! Shut the fuck—"

She swung her left elbow into Santiago's exposed midriff. He fell forward, and she wrenched free of his grip. She ran, tumbled, rolled away from him. He aimed his weapon at her.

"Fire! Now!" The command roared through Spann's ears. He ripped off a barrage of bullets that echoed in the warehouse. The shots rattled Lorraine's teeth and cut at nerve endings already worn down. She screamed and scratched at the concrete in a frantic effort to bury herself.

Santiago Jiménez twitched in a pool of blood.

A rough hand lifted Lorraine Garza and rushed her to an armored van.

Danny Mora and Robert Spann met for what they agreed would be the last time.

The office hadn't changed since the first time the two men had talked in the room. The masks stared at the immigration officer, neither revealing themselves nor offering solace. The bookshelves were crammed with the books that Spann thought had quirky titles. A thin layer of dust on the cherry wood shelves convinced Spann that Mora hadn't had much time for reading lately.

They didn't engage in any small talk. Spann had come to expect that from Mora, and so he started in almost immediately, providing the details about what had happened since Jiménez had been killed and Lorraine Garza arrested.

"She's talked until she's hoarse. Uh, sorry about that. Names, addresses, routes, connections, guys on the take, on both sides of the border. Feds in Texas, California, Arizona, and all along the border have busted coyotes, drug smugglers, caches of weapons. She's getting more than even for Kiko Vigil. The Cardoza operations have been hurt seriously. It just means that others are moving in. Mexicans, Colombians. Who knows what else. We're tracking a group of Russians who think they can get in on this. And plenty of outfits from the States ready to pick up the pieces."

Spann had trouble hearing Mora's bruised voice.

"And everyone's convinced that Garza's dead?" The words were dry, brittle.

Spann spoke carefully. "Not necessarily. We've heard about the death of Elías Garza before. Could be another cover-up, an escape, a red herring, easy. We're leery, naturally. A body was found stuffed in a Guadalajara sewer, and from what was left, the Mexican federal police tell us that they're sure it's Garza. Word's just getting out on the grapevine."

Danny said, "The news about Garza should hit Denver any hour now. That will make some people very nervous. Nervous enough to run or panic."

Spann agreed. "Sure. And Garza's killing makes sense, when you think about it. Cardoza needed to cut his losses. Like firing a manager for a losing baseball team, except in this business, the fired employee ends up without eyes, hands, or testicles."

Again Spann had to lean toward Mora to decipher the torn sound of his words.

Painfully Danny said, "That's about it for you, then, isn't it? Garza is history, Lorraine Garza is locked up and probably works a deal for her cooperation. Kiko Vigil's last case is finally closed."

Spann nodded. "Yeah. It's about as final as I can get it. Lorraine will tell us everything about Kiko—the good and the bad. But from what she's said so far, it's clear Kiko was killed because his cover had been blown. Garza wouldn't let personal issues jeopardize business. In fact, according to Lorraine, he would have let the affair continue if it would have helped business. Kiko could have been very valuable alive, if he had turned. Garza knew he wouldn't, and so he had him killed."

Mora asked, "And the killers? What about them?" He was patient.

"Lorraine says the triggermen were Jiménez and someone they called Fidel. She hasn't given us much on that guy so far. She's keeping a few things to herself, insurance, I guess. We figure she wants to be sure Garza is really dead before she shows her complete hand. Just a matter of time. We're not pushing it since what we are getting from her is better than gold."

Spann waited for a response, but Mora remained silent. The agent continued, "I guess the way it played out, we would have learned this sooner or later. Lorraine Garza had her own agenda. She's the one that will set this straight. All because of Kiko Vigil." He paused, cleared his throat. "I am sorry about your friend. If I hadn't come to you . . ." He let it go. Mora's face was blank.

Spann finished, "Send me your final bill and I'll take care of it. Includes that grand for the reward, right? That guy did help, didn't he?"

Mora nodded.

Spann stood up to leave. Mora turned his dark eyes directly on him. Spann waited.

Mora spoke slowly, as clearly as he could. "Your friend's reputation ends up being what it always was. A good cop who made bad choices about bad women. You didn't expect me to fix that, did you?"

"Well, there can't be much done about that. You looked into it. Hell, man, you almost got killed. You played a part in bringing this all to closure. You got something you can take to the cops to help find the killer of your friend—that weird Billy's ID."

Danny said, "Kiko Vigil did a good job of covering his ass. Anyway, for me, it falls together, hard as it may be for you to swallow. Not that I can prove anything."

"What are you talking about?" Spann hesitated. He didn't want to say too much.

"It was chancy, don't you think?" Mora cleared his throat again. "What if I had been able to get to the bottom of those killings in the desert? What if I had been able to link Kiko Vigil to the dead illegals?"

Spann's Adam's apple jumped.

Mora's voice had grown stronger as he talked. "But the risk was worth it for you, I guess."

He pressed on.

"I doubt you know the whole truth. For your own reasons you needed to confirm your suspicions about Kiko, about what happened in the middle of the night, in the desert, where it's too easy to get carried away. Where thousands of people cross the border every damn night and that eats at your cop insides. Where you can see that there's no stopping it. Anybody might lose it out there.

Before anyone really knows what's happening the shooting starts, and then it can't be stopped."

Spann looked away. He heard Mora say, "You added that newspaper story to the file. That's what this was all about. Tomás tried to tell me that your reasons for hiring me were weak. I should have listened to him. Instead I let him down."

He stopped, rested his throat. His words were thin wires, stretched to the breaking point. "It's torn you up. Not knowing for sure. Now you can rest easy. I didn't find any direct link between Kiko Vigil and what happened in the desert that night. I can't help you anymore, Robert."

Spann sputtered. He faced Mora.

"That's the wildest thing I've ever heard. You need some rest, Mora."

He ran out of the office and slammed the door.

Danny Mora opened the file that contained the yellowed news clipping about the people who had been found dead in the Arizona desert. The headline read, BODIES DISCOVERED NEAR ABANDONED MINE. The story mentioned that agent Francisco Vigil of the INS had been called in to help with the investigation.

The story had worked on Mora's imagination since the first time he had plucked it from Vigil's "research" file. The content wasn't that remarkable. Death on the road to *el norte* had become commonplace, especially for an agent like Vigil. The story obviously had been read through many times. Red ink marked a few of the paragraphs and a corner of the story had been torn, as though someone had carried it in his back pocket for days or folded up in a wallet. Kiko Vigil might have been that person, but

Mora doubted it. Vigil's newspaper clippings were neatly arranged on stiff backing. They were marked by date and source, prepared for possible use as exhibits in courtroom hearings. Out of an entire file of stories, only this one was different, only this one told Mora that he should pay special attention to it.

■

Danny had worried about Patricia after she had been sent home from the hospital, but that changed as soon as he saw the informal bodyguards who had set up camp in front of her house. He met them and they introduced themselves—sons, nephews, and cousins of friends of Carlos Montelibre who had been ordered by their fathers to protect Patricia. They tried to pat down Danny the first time he showed up, but Patricia put an end to that and prevented what might have turned into an ugly altercation in her front yard.

She moved slowly, with pain. The shattered tendon would never be the same, and her arm had become a lifeless piece of meat that served no good. Still, she was alive. So many others had died.

Danny Mora sipped on lemonade from a pitcher in her refrigerator. She surprised herself at how quickly she had become accustomed to Danny helping himself in her house.

Danny Mora had been her only regular visitor. Silvia and her friends—Carmen, Genevieve—had come by, once, and left quickly. Silvia's lecture about Patricia's childish mistakes, including her continued association with Danny Mora, fell on impatient ears. The gulf between the two had widened into an ocean by the time the three cleverly dressed, heavily accessorized women exited Patricia's house, sadly shaking their heads in unison.

Patricia said to Danny, "That witness, the man in the wheelchair. He picked this Fidel out of a picture. He killed the agent and Tomás. Do you know him?"

"I didn't recognize the man. There's something, but not enough. It was an old picture, bad quality. Garza and this Fidel were trying to cover up, stay out of camera range. Spann thinks it won't be long until he turns up. Probably dead. Lorraine Garza has been turning everyone in, from drivers to dealers in the parks, to honchos back in Guadalajara. The guy's either on the run or in jail. I'll talk with a police detective this afternoon. Show him the photo and the statement from Billy Cordero."

She reached for his hand. "Don't put it off. I can't be as cavalier about this as you."

"Yeah, sure. At least Cordero got his reward. He and his buddy were happy about that."

He scanned the photographs sitting on the top of a bookcase. Family, friends, pets. The usual. A black-and-white Polaroid sat toward the back of the row of colorful picture frames. Unframed, covered with a thin layer of dust, it rested against another, larger picture of Patricia and her friends, arms around each other's shoulders as they stood in line, staring at the camera. Danny picked up the black and white.

"Carlos?"

Patricia reached for the picture.

"Yes. I haven't looked at that for months. Almost forgot I still had it. Carlos, Alfred, and Inés, the day before the explosion at the house. Need to put it in an album. It's getting cracked."

Danny held out his hand, and Patricia returned the photo to him. Carlos, in the middle, with bushy hair around his shoulders. At one side, a woman dressed in jeans and a T-shirt that proclaimed: Free the Puerto Rican Four! The third person was another man, intense or glum, Danny couldn't decide, eyes looking off to the side.

Danny Mora grimaced. He shook his head.

"Sonofabitch."

It was more a prayer than a curse.

"What? What do you see?"

Without answering, he rushed to the dining-room table, where he had set down a manila file. It was for the police, later, when he planned to show the homicide detectives the photograph from which Frankie Johns had recognized the killer of Kiko Vigil. He pulled out the photograph and compared it with Patricia's.

"It's him."

He handed both pictures to Patricia. She glanced briefly at the scene of the rainy afternoon in Mexico City.

She wrinkled her face. "Who? What should I see?"

Mora pointed at the photo. "The guy in the umbrella. He's in the picture with your brother. Much younger, of course, but it's him."

Patricia moved the picture closer to her eyes. "That can't be. Alfred Leal was killed in the explosion, along with Carlos and Inés. And this man in your picture, he's older, alive. Must be . . ."

She dropped the picture, and it fluttered to the ground.

Mora said, "It's Garza. Leal turned into Garza. He's dead now. Can't do anything else to us. He must have been a snitch or an agent, spying on your brother and his friends.

Happened all the time in those days. He probably set off the explosion. People think he died, too. Then he's dumped in witness protection, given a new life. He lands in Mexico. Bad from the beginning to the end. He's finally gone. I'm sorry, I didn't mean to upset you."

She nodded, then shook her head. She cried out, "I don't understand all of it. But Danny. That other man, in the picture, walking away. I know that man."

23

Eugene Nieto gripped the steering wheel as though it were a life preserver and he was a drowning man.

Shit is flowing over, and I'm going to get sucked into it. Drowning ain't the least of it. Got to do something. Take care of this now. That Garza woman is taking everyone down with her. Fidel will be next. She's saving him for last, something special. He'll crack. He'll pin the whole fucking mess on me, and all I did, all I really did, was a simple slowing down of that case, mucking up the Vigil thing. But it's enough. That sonofabitch detective is wise. With him and Fidel, and what they know, I could do some time. The joint is no place for a cop. No place for me.

He had always known Fidel as Fidel, but that name had never really mattered to Nieto. It had been a silly ruse for others. Eugene Nieto and Fidel weren't strangers. They were practically homeboys, *carnales,* like those wiseass punks from the projects talked about. Eugene knew the man and where he could be found, if he hadn't run yet.

The trip took only a few minutes from the District 1 station house. The multiblock renewal project included a coffee shop, a deli, bookstores, a gourmet burrito diner, and Casa Fernández, Carmen and Reymundo Fernández's pride and joy. The Highlands neighborhood had been made over, upgraded. It was where Nieto would find his man.

Have to straighten this out so that I don't get caught in a squeeze. Feel him out, test him for weakness. If he's going to break, then what? What do I do? Whatever I have to.

He drove west on Thirty-second until he intersected with Lowell Boulevard. Casa Fernández was one block over, on Meade Street.

He drove in the alley behind the shop and parked the car. He walked to the back door of the shop, where he heard the noise. Boxes crashed, figurines smashed against the floor, glass objects cracked and splintered. He drew his weapon and ran through the wide-open back door.

Two bloody men were fighting. Reymundo Fernández threw a punch at Danny Mora that landed on his jaw. Mora fell backward and slammed into a display of two-feet-high papier-mâché skeletons wearing Mexican sombreros and holding toy rifles. His head hit the edge of a wrought-iron table. Reymundo advanced to the fallen man.

Shelves and racks of clothes were turned over, and pieces of broken pottery, ceramic statues, and clay figurines were strewn across the floor.

Both men bled from cuts on the face, and a large purple knot extruded from Fernández's forehead. Mora looked passed out.

Reymundo pulled a gun from his waist. He aimed at Mora.

Nieto said, "What the hell are you doing?" He lifted his gun and pointed it at Fernández, but he didn't shoot. He didn't want to make more noise than had already drifted out to the street. Any minute now another police cruiser would screech to a stop in front of Casa Fernández. He had to be ready.

Reymundo Fernández wobbled unsteadily. His torn and twisted face glared at the policeman. He smiled at the gun in the policeman's hand.

"Nieto? Finally came by to see me, eh? Thought I might have to leave without saying good-bye. Two surprises in one day. First this meddling fucker, now you. Well, I'm on my way out of town, for good. As soon as I deal with this." He turned his head toward Mora.

"Don't," Nieto said. "There's no need."

Fernández looked back at the cop. "No need? Are you serious? This guy knows everything, pendejo! From Vigil to Delgado to Chávez to who knows what the fuck else. With what Lorraine is feeding the cops and this guy, I have no choice. It's my ass, man. I knew that bitch Lorraine would screw it up for everybody. And you think there's no need to finish off this guy? Remember, Eugene, he's got your number, too."

Reymundo returned his attention to Danny Mora. He aimed his gun. A shot echoed in the store. Nieto flinched. Reymundo crumpled to his knee. Blood flowed from his chest and onto the broken and smashed remnants of his business. He collapsed, flat on his back.

Danny Mora sat up, his fingers limply holding a gun.

The cut on his forehead was ugly and deep, and blood smeared his face. He sat there, not moving, not doing anything, too dazed to see clearly or understand all that had happened.

Officer Nieto picked up Reymundo Fernández's gun. He surveyed the broken store, the street, the back door. He placed the gun in the dead man's hand. Nieto squeezed the dead man's fingers. A bullet exploded into the sagging body of Danny Mora. Nieto dropped the gun and stepped away from the two bodies.

He walked out the back door and used the radio in his car.

"This is Patrolman Eugene Nieto at the Casa Fernández at Meade and Thirty-second. Emergency. Shots fired. Need an ambulance. Two men down. Hurry, it looks bad."

Autumn hung around the corner, waiting for the last few days of the dried-out, strung-out, wiped-out summer to finally pack it in, to end it all. The heat had been beaten back again, and this time the promise in the air breathed of cooler, damper hours, long, jealous nights, and gray, unforgiving days.

The flower seller paraded back and forth all around his corner, twisting and gyrating to the music from his compatriot, who sat in a wheelchair, blowing and fingering a tarnished saxophone as though he had taken the stage at Newport, as though he were warming up the crowd for Sonny Rollins. The flower seller sported purple Air Jordans, so expensive that the flower seller couldn't even imagine the sum needed to buy such a luxury, and, consequently, all those details had been left to his friend, the musician, who wore a fancy, tooled leather harness around his neck, hooked up to his trusty old ax.

That was the way it had to be, if the flower seller dared to tell the story of the purchases that one day, when it was still Hades hot, when the sun cooked eyeballs and tongues, when water tasted sweeter than honey, and the musician had collected his well-earned reward. First thing he did, wouldn't you know, he took care of his friend, sidled right on up to that shoe store, if *sidle* was the right word for directing the wheelchair where it needed to be, and let that young man in the black-and-white-striped shirt know right off that they needed a couple of pairs of those famous shoes that Michael Jackson wore. The man laughed, they always laughed, those kind of men with no shine in their eyes, but in the end the flower seller and the musician had their shoes, and the flower seller had never felt lighter on his feet, had never soared with the birds the way he could after he strapped on those purple babies, after he did his dance on the street in his new shoes.

And the music! Who would have thought that a simple thing like a new strap for resting the machine across the neck and chest could change an attitude, could alter the course of melodies and lyrics, could stir up the fires of a man who had almost lost the flare in his heart?

There was something about the woman; the flower seller could tell that right off. She held her left arm close to her chest, afraid to move it, or maybe she couldn't move it, maybe it was locked that way forever, a halfhearted wave of hello, or the first step in a handshake, frozen and thwarted in mimicry of elegant motion.

The musician changed his riff, went from bebop

kinetics to slowly sifted sadness. He played "Fine and Mellow," the Billie Holiday tune that he tried to avoid because it made his throat tight, because the ironic anguish in the melody played kick ball with his heart. There was no avoiding the song that afternoon, it couldn't be turned away, and the musician decided that when he had no choice in these matters, he played his best anyway, and that's what it was all about, wasn't it?

"I'll take two bunches of those yellow roses, please."

Her voice is blue and misty, like a teardrop.

The flower seller prepared the order with extra pizzazz, because he liked this pretty lady, even if she was awful sad, and there were only so many things he could do for customers he liked, and pizzazz was right at the top of that list.

The musician stopped playing, and the corner went dry, the air limp and thin, and the flower seller hoped that the musician would start again soon. It was always better when he played, when he turned loose the notes that freed the songs.

The musician said, "For a couple of friends?"

She tightened the scarf at her neck. She had noticed the change, too. She tried to smile when she said, "Chacho and Moony. That's their names. Chacho and Moony."

David and Billy said, in unison, "Chacho and Moony?"

David the Dancer immediately imagined a new step that would take advantage of the rhythms in the words *Chacho* and *Moony*. And Billy Cordero, who called himself Frankie, concluded Chacho and Moony were a pair of grand names. Grand names, indeed.